C000003386

Mika Ito

Published 2022

ISBN 979-8-836752-02-6

Printed by Amazon KDP

Cover design by Agata Bukovero
bukovero.com

Edited by Louise Harnby
louiseharnbyproofreader.com

Proofread by Kim Kimber (kimkimber.co.uk) and Peri Turner

Typeset by The Book Typesetters
thebooktypesetters.com

MIKA ITO

PETER FOLEY

'The mass of men lead lives of quiet desperation.'

– Henry David Thoreau

ONE

I t was 11 a.m. when Dylan Solly collapsed in Yonomori Park, and no matter what, he'd unlikely ever forget the rhythm of that cold March Friday morning. The day had started easy, but a call from his editor picked up the beat.

'Not again, Sam.'

'I know it's a lot earlier than we discussed, but I've got nothing for the next issue so I need your report ASAP.'

Dylan fumbled with the ring hanging from his necklace. 'The Notorious Three trial hasn't even started yet, and these guys are way above the usual Yakuza criminal enterprise. This thing goes deep and international, so it's worth taking our time. If we do this right, it'll be another award winner.'

'I'm sorry, no. Look, you'll get the story – I know you will. You always find a way. And, yes, there's a lot of ground to cover on this one but I can get Kasper on the next plane to Japan to help you with the research. Let me send you an assistant—'

'No. You'll get your story.'

Dylan hung up, reached for his cigarettes and slipped a notebook into his pocket. Then he grabbed his wallet and his old Nikon and headed out into the cool air of the park, where the melody of his late-morning anxiety climaxed.

A jagged scar appeared across his vision, narrowing the view of the bright blossoms. The pressure in his skull built. He pitched forward and the camera slipped from his hands. Newly cut grass squashed under his palms as he met the ground.

He rolled onto his back.

The sun transformed into a halo of scattered phosphorus pink, violet and gold. That's when he saw her, looming over him, blocking the harsh light. While rings of purple orbited her, Dylan passed out.

TWO

Dylan woke with a jolt, lungs empty, brain foggy. The sky looked different somehow. Low and still.

Not sky. A high ceiling, decorated with thick brush strokes of cerulean and coarse white – like an abstract spring heaven. He lay on a couch overpopulated with pillows. Across the room, velvet curtains buffeted on cool air blowing through a balcony window, beyond which he could see the park. The sun painted a column of amber light across a polished oak floor. A harp sat in one corner. Above it, a print of Mount Fuji coloured in red hung on the wall. Opposite, a bookcase brimmed with neat, colourful spines.

The woman from the park appeared beside him, holding a glazed porcelain tumbler. Steam leapt from the cup and danced around her shoulder-length silky brown hair. Tiger eyes glinted.

'Konnichiwa. Taichou wa dou? Amari yokunai tte? Sorejaa, kore wo nonde. Matcha yo. Korewo nomeba genki ni nareru wa,' she said. 'Sukoshi yasumeba daijoubu datte oishasan ga ittetawa.'

She gestured with the cup, and he took it. Their fingers touched briefly, and an energy passed between them.

What the hell had he gotten himself into this time?

He was only thirty-three for Christ's sake, yet he felt old, broken, unable to muster the charisma such a situation required.

'Hi! I'm Dylan Solly,' he muttered. 'And I speak no Japanese. So,

3

yeah, thanks for the tea, but I've no idea what you just said and I'm fairly certain you can't understand me either. Frankly, I could be talking complete gibberish for all you know. I could be telling you about the time I fell prey to a prank involving super glue and a toilet seat, or I might even be saying how beautiful you are, and how, if I had the courage—'

She burst out laughing. 'You think I don't speak English? How rude!'

Dylan felt his cheeks flush. 'Sorry, that wasn't my intention. Although that's not the first time I've been told I come across that way.' He sipped the tea, hoping it would mask his blushes. 'It's just that there aren't many English speakers around here.'

'You should never assume.' She shook her head, but the smile stayed on her lips. 'My name is Mika Ito. I teach English at the school. The tea is a matcha – it will perk you up a little. The doctor said you'll be fine after some rest.'

'Thank you for your help. I feel okay now, just slightly out of place and a bit of a burden.' He toyed with the ring on his necklace again. 'Did you bring me up here alone?'

'Pretty much. The doctor helped a little, but you're not that heavy, just a dead weight. Is there anyone you need to call?'

Dead weight? What did that mean? He brushed over the comment. 'I suppose I could do with gaining a few pounds. Wait, I had a camera. Did you see it?'

'It's over there.'

The Nikon sat on a side table. It was smeared with dirt, and the lens was broken.

'I think it's smashed.'

'Damn! I'll have to find a repair shop.'

'What happened?'

'I blacked out. I get headaches. Some are worse than others. That was a bad one, I guess. A really bad one.'

'You need to be careful. You could have been left in the park all day.

People would have assumed you were drunk, homeless or dangerous.'

'I appreciate your assistance, but I'm fine now. I'll get out of your hair.' He tried to pull himself up but hadn't the strength.

'Calm down,' she said. 'The doctor said you need to rest, so drink your tea. You're from England?'

'Yeah.' He lay back.

'And you don't speak any Japanese?'

'Correct.'

'How can you survive in Japan without knowing the language?'

Again, he tried to sit up, and this time succeeded. 'I get by with a phrase book, and I hire the occasional translator. I'm only here for a week or so anyway. I'm writing an article for a magazine back home. My name's Dylan Solly. You might have heard of me.'

'No. You're writing about Tomioka?'

'I'm covering the trial of the Notorious Three—'

'The Three?' She perched on the edge of the couch. 'That's dangerous, and pretty stupid to do that on your own. The Three kill people.'

'I'm not always by myself, like I told you already. I pick up a local translator for a few hours here and there to assist me. And the work isn't dangerous. I'm just covering a trial. It's mostly going through records, witness accounts, police reports, things like that. There's a lot to go through, a decade's worth of data. And there's plenty of folks to interview, too.'

'You do all that alone? Why?'

'You sound like my editor. She's always trying to partner me up with a photographer or an assistant. She doesn't understand that I'm not interested.'

'If I were you, and I had all that work, I'd take the help.'

'But you're not me and I don't need help. Besides, I realised a long time ago that I can look after myself, but no one else. I don't want the grief.'

'You never stick your neck out for anyone, huh?' Mika raised an eyebrow.

5

'It's not like that.'

'What is it like?'

He took another sip of matcha. 'So you've heard of the Notorious Three?'

'Everyone around here knows about the Three. They've terrorised this village for years.' She shook her head. 'The children tease each other with stories about them, but for everyone else they're no joke.'

The local angle. Always newsworthy. Dylan set down his cup and reached into his pocket for the notepad. 'Have you lived here long?'

'My whole life. I've only ever left Tomioka once, to go on holiday with my parents when I was young. They took me to this amazing park up north – it's so beautiful there. If you ever get a chance, you should go. It has natural springs, crater lakes and lots of wildlife. I think I have pictures somewhere, unless my mom took them all with her. Let me see, they might still be over here.' She got up and walked over to the bookshelf. 'I'm sure I still have that photo album ...'

'What do you know about the trial?' Dylan said.

'Trial?'

'You haven't heard? It's pretty massive news. It's all over the international media.'

'I choose *not* to follow such things.'

Dylan sighed, pocketed the notepad and checked his phone. While Mika riffled through her bookshelf, he gave her the news. 'There's enough evidence to prosecute the Three for everything from sexual slavery, to human trafficking, murder, blackmail, and the distribution of drugs. And that's just the start. The real news will come when the verdict's announced. I'm here to see what moves the judge makes. Rumours are, the Three can't be touched because they have so many people in their pockets. I'm going to find out who, so I can expose them for what they are – enablers and accessories after the fact.'

'Where is it?' Mika muttered, rummaging through a drawer.

'And as for the leader, they call him the Tomioka Torturer. Have you heard about him? He's a real sicko. Has a fetish for kidnapping.

He holds people captive and destroys their minds, usually with a combination of drugs, starvation, pain and sleep deprivation. According to the tabloids, he calls it *research* into the limits of the human mind and body. Then he burns them alive – what remains of them anyway. And he has a thing for amputation—'

'That's enough!' Mika raised her hand. 'I don't want to hear any more. I live a very peaceful life as an English teacher. On purpose. I won't have you ruin that.'

'Cute. I wish I'd kept it simple. Too late for that now though. I've been chasing stories for too long. It's what I do. I'm a professional.'

Mika returned to the couch. 'No wonder you get headaches – work, work, work, stories, stories, stories. Take a break.'

'No chance.'

She rolled her eyes.

'I mean it,' he said. 'I'll likely never stop, ever. Though I honestly wish I could.' He paused, feeling like a poker player who'd just let his bluff slip. Maybe it was time to fold. Terrible things happened to people every day and nobody batted an eyelid. Perhaps she really didn't care.

He did though. And that was enough.

'Truth is, I hate this goddamn job, and I've been doing it far longer than I care to admit. Ten, twelve years maybe. I should have stepped away early on, but I got too used to the money and now I can't get out and I think it's killing me.'

'Are all Englishmen so dramatic? If you hate your job, quit. I can't imagine being in that position.'

'I can't bring myself to. It's become all I am. It consumes me, like a bad habit. Maybe there was a time I could've cut back, found a new job, but I didn't, and it's too late now. It's been too late for five damn years.'

Had it been that long already? It seemed like it had only happened yesterday. It never left his mind.

'What's so special about five years ago?'

'Back then, 2006, I was … Wait, what's that? What's that noise?'

The floor started to vibrate and the whole room started to hum. On the wall, Mount Fuji trembled, jerked and fell. Books danced off the shelves, his teacup skidded across the table, and the harp crashed to the floor with a discordant clang. Mika tumbled on top of him. A cacophony of screams and car alarms erupted in the streets outside.

Then the building started to sway.

What the hell?

THREE

D ylan stumbled to the window. A woman carrying a child ran down the road as hundreds of birds took to the sky amid the cracking and rumbling. Water vented from the town fountain. The road's surface snaked and split. A statue crashed to the ground and broke into pieces, kicking a cloud of dust over the mother and child. The plume rose, creating a haze over a line of overhead power cables that whipped viciously through the air.

The apartment walls ruptured in zig-zag lines. Light bulbs shattered and cupboards spilled their contents onto the floor. Frightened cries from neighbouring rooms came through the walls as the building flexed and groaned.

For the next six minutes, Dylan knelt, face to face, eye to eye with Mika, convinced her face was the last he'd see, sure that this was the end of the world, or at least the end of his.

And then, in an instant, the subterranean ripples disappeared, and the screams and car alarms quieted.

'I think we're okay,' Mika said.

She broke away from Dylan's gaze and looked around the apartment. The place was trashed.

Dylan's breathless relief was shattered by a banging at the door and a muffled voice beyond. Mika's expression went from furrowed brow to eye roll.

'It's Itsumi, my neighbour. I don't know why she knocks. She knows my door's always open.'

An elderly woman wearing slippers, a thick pink housecoat and a yellow headscarf burst into the room. She yelled what sounded to Dylan like the same sentence over and over again in varying tones, then darted around the room until she came to him. She stopped and stared.

'Hi!' he said.

Itsumi resumed her worried barrage, and Mika offered calming words and a long hug, then approached the TV.

'Let's see if we have any electricity.'

To Dylan's surprise, the screen came to life. He got up and stood by Mika as the news anchor spoke in a deep, grave tone. Images from across Japan spoke for themselves – the Akua high-rise swaying in Tokyo, Yuriage Bridge snapping in Natori City, and CCTV from inside the news station's office showing ceiling tiles falling on employees hiding under desks.

The anchor spoke again, and Itsumi's lament resumed, this time laced with even more anguish.

'What did he just say?' Dylan asked.

'Shush!' Mika said, turning up the volume.

'What's going on? We're okay, right? We just survived a massive bloody earthquake.'

Mika pulled out her phone, her expression morphing into terror as she tapped the screen.

'For crying out loud, what is it?' he said.

Mika looked up. The white glow from the phone lit up her face as she whispered just a single word.

'Tsunami.'

FOUR

'Should we run?' Dylan asked.

'No.'

Mika paced the floor, her iPhone pressed to her ear. Dylan sat on the couch and called the magazine's head office on his BlackBerry. No answer.

Mika ended her call and dialled again. There was a quick exchange, then she hung up and faced him. 'The latest alert says the waves are expected to be three metres high. We're on the fifth floor – way above the threshold. This is a modern building, one of the tallest in town. It's strong.'

'So we're just going to sit here? Is that wise?'

Mika went over to Itsumi and tried to calm her. Dylan texted Sam, his editor: *CALL ME. NOW!*

'We should leave and get to higher ground,' he said.

'The east of Tomioka is all flat land, and we're in the east,' Mika said. 'There's no place above sea level for miles. And we can't get out of town because the news says the highway's blocked. The only other place to go is the school.'

'Why there?'

'It was designed as a gathering point for the town. It can withstand the forces of an earthquake and the structure's tsunami-proof. There's a refuge on the top floor that can hold a thousand people. I'm trying to reach as many parents as I can and tell them to head there if they have nowhere else to go. The waves could be here any minute.'

She dashed around the apartment, stuffing items into a rucksack – phone charger, purse, first-aid kit, water bottle, blanket. She grabbed car keys from a bowl near the door and pushed them deep into her pocket.

'What do you need those for?' Dylan said. 'You just said we can't go anywhere.'

'Superstition.'

'I never heard of that superstition before.'

'Because I just made it up.' She slipped the bag over her shoulders. 'We'll be fine up here, but it doesn't hurt to be prepared.'

Her phone rang again.

'Sure,' Dylan said. 'What can I do to help?'

She let out a sharp breath. 'Pray.'

FIVE

Mika put the phone to her ear. The voice on the other end was distorted and broken.

'Mika. It's your mother. Listen to me. You're in danger. You have to leave Tomioka at once.'

'Mom, I can't! The highway's blocked.'

'I never should have left you in that town on your own. My poor pudding cake—'

'I wish you wouldn't call me that! I'm twenty-six years old.'

'So young and trapped in Tomioka all alone – with a tsunami coming! You could be swept out into the ocean! As if the earthquake wasn't bad enough. Even here it caused a mess. I know you're a warrior, just like your grandmother, but come to Cape Sōya and be with your mother. It's beautiful here and you'll be safe.'

'Cape Sōya is a twenty-two-hour drive. Besides, my apartment is safe, Mom, and I want to stay here for my students. They'll need me once this is over.'

'I was a teacher too, remember? Of course, I had to give all that up for you, but, believe me, those children have parents who can look after them very well without you. You don't need to stay on their account.'

Mika moved into the bedroom and mouthed expletives at the ceiling.

'Why did you just move into your bedroom?' Opere said.

'How did you know?'

'It has that empty echo to it. Now come and look after your mother.'

'You're going to be fine, and I'm going to be fine.'

'I have a fire ready for you.'

Mika could hear her mother stoking hot coals in the hearth. Her own apartment felt suddenly cold.

'You can't stay there all by yourself.'

'I'm not alone.'

'I hardly think that old neighbour of yours will be of any use in an emergency like this.'

'She's fine, and there's somebody else here.'

The fire poker clanged to the floor. 'Is it a man? It's a man, isn't it? You have a man in your apartment? Who knows about him? How long has this been going on?'

'Calm down. Nothing's going on. Nothing at all.'

'If you're involved with somebody I need to know. Don't keep secrets from your mother.'

Mika perched on the bed. 'Mom, you caught me – I have fifty boyfriends, and I sleep with them every day. Happy now?'

'Don't joke, Mika!'

'It's just some English guy, but—'

'Has anyone seen you with him?'

'It doesn't matter. I'm not dating him, or anyone else for that matter. He had an accident in the park this morning, and I helped him.'

'I do wish you could lead a normal romantic life.'

'If you'd leave me to it then maybe I would. I'm fine, Mom. I'm hanging up now. Love you. Bye.'

'But Mika—'

She ended the call. There were more important things to attend to. Like the wave that could hit them at any moment.

SIX

Dylan waited, his nerves frayed. He sat, and when that brought no comfort, he paced. The TV continued to broadcast news about a tide that was sweeping thousands of people into the ocean. Mika, still with her backpack on, made more calls, encouraging parents to take their children to the school's top-floor safehouse.

Maybe the news reports were wrong. He picked up his broken camera and checked to see if it powered on.

Then the TV cut out and the lights went off.

The world outside became strangely overcast.

It had been forty-one minutes since Mika uttered the word 'tsunami'. Now, on the horizon, what looked like smoke rolled over the trees.

Only there was no fire.

It was the spray from the oncoming wave front.

The water was coming.

Glasses, plates and cutlery started to shake and clink on the floor. The harp danced and hummed in an agonising pitch.

'We're not high enough,' Dylan whispered. 'We need to get higher.'

The wave hurtled towards the apartment, bringing with it cars, boats, concrete blocks, metal girders, rooftops ...

'Hold on!' Mika shouted.

The wave hit the building with a roar. Mika and Itsumi stumbled and fell, and Dylan gripped the edge of the doorframe as filthy water bled into the living room from under the door and up through the floorboards.

The cold, dirty swell rose above his knees, quickening his breath and lifting Mika and Itsumi off their feet. His fingers slipped, and he was dragged into the swirling room.

Mika and Itsumi choked and sank.

Dylan prayed then – that it wouldn't get any higher, that the structure would hold, that they'd live.

He tilted his head back, drew a lungful of air, and plunged beneath the rank water. It flooded his sinuses as he reached out in the cold, murky dark to Mika and Itsumi.

There was a sudden, muffled crack. His head rose above the torrent for just a moment. An exterior wall buckled and collapsed into the park below, and he was submerged once more. Then he was spiralling. There was no sense of up or down. No light. No air. Just the monstrous ocean.

SEVEN

'Do you see Itsumi?' Mika said.

Mika was struggling to stay afloat, so Dylan hooked his arms around her. They settled, shivering, in a stew of mud, froth and splintered wood as the dim sky swirled overhead. Dylan tried not to look at the bodies.

'Are you okay?' he said.

'I'm hurt. My leg. Itsumi. Do you see her?'

Dylan scanned the water. 'I'm sorry, I don't.'

'We have to find her.'

'I think she's gone.'

A remnant of what looked like Mika's bookcase floated by. Dylan pulled her towards it, and they clung to it and each other.

In the distance, the top floor of the school peeked above the flood. Mika called out to Itsumi, but the only response was the roll of the sea.

Gradually, the devil waters receded, and Dylan felt wet ground beneath his feet. He scoured the land. Each part of Tomioka told its own tale. In some areas the undertide had folded the earth and washed it bare, leaving behind long, winding scars. Half a sightseeing boat lay on top of a two-storey office block. A fishing vessel leant against a storefront, surrounded by a wide bed of rubble and broken planks. Lorries and cars were piled on top of one another. Smoke from the corner of an upturned building billowed high in the air, and across the vista small fires coloured the world orange and black.

Mika's backpack was gone. Dylan's camera had suffered the same fate, and his mobile was soaked and refused to power up. He tossed it aside and rummaged in his pockets. His notebook and cigarettes were sodden, the wallet too. He flicked open the Zippo and flicked the flint wheel. It lit. 'Least that still works.'

'Are you crazy?' Mika shouted into the rising night. 'Who cares?' She wiped tears from her silt-stained face. 'Look. Just look.'

Dylan followed her gaze. Amid the carnage, people held themselves and rocked.

And then the ground began to rumble again.

EIGHT

Dylan lost his footing and fell to his knees. The rumble got louder. Not the earth's crust and mantle colliding in the Pacific this time. The thrum of rotor blades.

Mika cupped her hands and yelled up into the twilight sky as three helicopters passed over. But the *thwump* soon faded, leaving a new and strange silence that was punctuated intermittently by distant wails carried on a faint breeze.

'We need to get the survivors together,' she said. 'They'll freeze to death on their own.'

She tripped and Dylan went to her. 'You can hardly walk. Let's stay here and wait for help.'

'No. We need to help the survivors.' She pulled wet strands of hair off her face and tried again to walk.

'Stop!' Dylan said. 'Look, I'll go and search. If I find anybody, I'll bring them here to you.'

Mika nodded. 'Go! Go find them!'

The town's landmarks and roads were unrecognisable, and he couldn't speak the language, meaning he'd have to rely on hand gestures. This wasn't going to be easy. He tramped across waterlogged streets and through furrows of wreckage. A heap of roofing tiles and metal avalanched, and he skittered to a safe distance. A familiar pressure mounted in his head and lanced through his temples. He reached up and raked at his neck. The necklace was intact.

Thank fuck. What a day.

The encroaching headache was milder than this morning's, like an echo or aftershock, and he tried to will it away by focusing on what he could hear. Nothing, but how many were entombed under the rubble, trapped in the dark? But there were no muffled voices, no yells or cries for help from within. The silence rendered him powerless, ashamed almost.

He pressed on and found a middle-aged woman in a muddy white dress cradling one arm.

'Come with me,' he said. 'I'll take you to a gathering point.'

The woman spoke. Dylan smiled and helped her to her feet while apologising for his lack of Japanese. She was frail and struggled to navigate the littered ground. Her hysteria mounted, and she only calmed when Mika came into view and called out her name. Mika embraced the woman – a Mrs Cho – and Dylan headed back out on his search.

He found a mother and father with a crying baby and brought them to the rendezvous point. Mika was addressing a group of people, so he left her to it and headed to the perimeter of one of the few buildings still upright. It was the town's courthouse – a three-storey concrete office block near Yonomori Park. The surrounding buildings had been reduced to their foundations.

Dylan circled around the back. While the courthouse's façade was intact, the rear had disintegrated. He heard a cry and hiked across the ruin. An old man was pinned to the ground by a huge steel girder. His eyes were shut and he grimaced as he tried to push the huge beam off his leg with blood-soaked hands.

Dylan stopped, trying to process what he was seeing.

Long grey hair. Round black glasses.

He knew this man, had written the story of his criminal career only this morning. And even though the man's face was creased in agony, there was no doubt.

It was none other than Shinsuke Takahashi, the Tomioka Torturer; leader of the Notorious Three.

NINE

The slight man redoubled his efforts, but the girder didn't budge. Dylan stayed in the shadows. Takahashi's dark eyes met his.

Dylan didn't need his spoiled notepad to refresh his memory. Takahashi was a dual citizen of Japan and Uruguay. The latter was where he'd studied his craft – in the late 1960s, long before the tabloids had nicknamed him. He'd been a disciple of Dan Mitrione, an American CIA operative who'd been appointed chief public safety advisor in Montevideo. At a time when the ruling Colorado Party faced daily riots due to the collapsing economy and the rise of a left-wing urban terror group – the Tupamaros – Takahashi had mastered the art of torture in the basement of Mitrione's suburban home, applying electric shocks to homeless people – test subjects, executed when the class was over. He'd graduated and become part of a task force that had crushed the Tupamaros through a relentless operation involving kidnap, torture, the extraction of false confessions and old-fashioned murder. Sometime around 1980, Dan Mitrione had been assassinated, and Uruguay became too hot. With the political climate shifting, Takahashi had gone underground, then moved to Tomioka and taken on a new identity as a clinician.

It was just a front. Behind the scenes, he was dedicating his life to studying how extreme trauma could turn victims into subordinates. His widened skillset included sleep deprivation, sensory overwhelm, mutilation and psychoactive drugs.

It was just the start.

He recruited Freddie Yoka and Jushin Okada, and the Three had indoctrinated a workforce of all-female agents and dispatched them across the world. Their role? To ensnare and compromise politicians, celebrities, big-tech owners and other masters of the universe. The plan had worked. They got dirt on everybody.

And yet the monster before Dylan appeared nothing short of a helpless old man, wailing and rocking, his bloody hands imploring, his wrinkled face begging.

What to do? Dylan could get a few survivors together and lift the load off his leg, at least enough for him to shuffle free. After all Takahashi had done, people would want to see justice served. They were owed that, weren't they?

Then Dylan recalled the case of a kidnapped teenager, three years prior.

That poor girl …

She'd woken up and found herself trapped in a wooden box no more than a metre long on each side, equipped with apparatus that could heat and cool the interior to extremes. It had been fitted with speakers and strobe lights that could be controlled externally. Takahashi's design. Devised to expose its occupants to a high-stress environment and measure how quickly their nervous systems collapsed.

The victim had eventually been discovered in the marshland outside Tomioka – alive, naked and covered in mud. It had taken her parents two years to teach her how to talk without breaking into screams. She'd described her captor as an old man with long silver hair and black glasses.

There'd been no reason for it other than Takahashi's fetish.

Dylan contemplated justice, and what it meant, then yelled across the ruined courthouse, 'The jury's in, Takahashi. Fuck you.'

He walked away, leaving the old man to die.

TEN

A truck rumbled in the distance. Mika waved frantically and called out to it. It turned and lumbered towards her, then stopped just short of where she stood. Huge white headlights floodlit the scene. Six soldiers exited the vehicle and unloaded bottles of water, neatly wrapped blankets and medical kits.

'A lot of people are missing and many are dead,' she said to one of the soldiers. 'We've been encouraging survivors to gather here.'

'It's the same along the entire coast. Are you okay? Do you need medical attention?'

She pointed to a weary couple sitting on the floor. 'This is Mr and Mrs Sato. He's diabetic and she's in shock.'

Mika, hobbling, led him through the small crowd to a family whose father was attempting to improvise a sling from his shirt. 'That's the Yamamoto family. Their daughter, Aimi, has a broken wrist. And over there in the purple coat is Mosu. He's having a bad time with the cold.' She pointed again. 'And Mrs Cho's hurt her elbow.'

'We've got it from here,' the serviceman said.

'I see you have blankets,' Mika said. 'I'll help to hand them out. Will there be more soldiers coming soon? Will you go to the school and look for other survivors?'

'I'm sorry, we're all that's coming for at least forty-eight hours. Our resources are spread thin. The whole country's affected. The rescue effort will move as quickly as our resources allow.'

'Mika.'

The accented voice was familiar.

'Dylan! Did you find anyone else?'

'No.'

She grabbed a blanket and wrapped it around him.

'You okay?'

She rubbed her eyes. 'I have to get to the school and make sure the children and the parents are okay.'

'The army's here. Let them check it out. You must be exhausted – I know I am.' He took the blanket from his shoulders and put it around her.

'No. I sent those children to the school building – I need to know they're alright. Look around – there's only a few soldiers and they have their hands full. I'm going to check for myself. It's only a twenty-minute walk.'

'And walking's a problem for you. You can hardly move on that ankle. I'm sure the army will coordinate passage to a safe location for everyone, and they'll check on the school in the process. Let's stay here and wait for transport.'

'I didn't say you had to come with me. I'm going.'

He bit his lip. 'Fine. I'll help you get there. It'll be a good angle on the story.'

Mika shook her head. 'This isn't a story, Dylan. It's a tragedy.'

The clouds gathered in the day's final light as Dylan helped Mika limp across the sodden ground. She lost her footing and grabbed his hand. He kept her upright, just about, and they walked on hand in hand. For Mika, it was practical; for Dylan, it was the unfamiliar warmth and the essence of trust bound in her soft grasp.

'Why do you do that?' Mika said.

'What?'

'Play with your shirt.'

'It's my necklace. I have a habit of messing with it.'

'Let me see.' She stopped, reached into his shirt and pulled out the chain.

'A ring?'

She peered at the etching, her face inches from his. '1997. What does that mean?'

'It's my friend's graduation ring. His name was Geoff. He used to say this ring was a reminder of privilege. He wanted me to have it.'

She said nothing, just nodded, urging him to continue.

'He died. Five years ago, almost to the week.'

'Tell me about five years ago.'

Dylan shrugged.

She pointed at his chest. 'Tell me.'

'It was June 7th, 2006, if you must know. We were working on a story in Iraq. Based on some bad information, we drove out to the university district of Baghdad to interview some students. I think we might have been set up by the translator … It all happened so quickly. We got out of our car. A van appeared at our side and a group of men jumped out. They put bags over our heads, threw us in and drove us away. It took seconds.'

'Kidnapped?'

'We were held for nine days in this little apartment on the edge of God knows where. They were the worst days of my life, but the magazine loved it. There's nothing like a crisis to boost circulation.'

She stared down at the battered bronze ring, her damp, dark hair moving in the cool breeze. 'What happened to Geoff?'

'Large chunks of my memory of those nine days are gone. I must have blocked a lot of it out, or been too concussed to remember. But one memory's clear. One of the kidnappers attacked me with a metal pipe. No surprise where my headaches come from. But Geoff, he was a warrior. He was just as beaten down as me, but he fought back, took the beating for me. Saved my life.'

Her eyes captured the sun's fading light. 'Go on.'

'Yeah, and I remember it like yesterday. The room was boiling hot. We were exhausted, dehydrated, half starved, but he kept fighting, kept trying to protect me. Then he just fell to the ground, clutching his chest. I can still see him lying across the room, taking off his ring, passing it to me. I'll never forgot that look in his eyes as he reached out across the floor.'

'He was a good friend.'

'I miss him ... Eventually, a ransom was paid by the magazine's parent company. That's how I got out. I don't know why it took them so long. Our captors dropped us on the street outside our hotel. I carried Geoff's body into the lobby.'

Mika put the ring back under his shirt.

'Powerful idiots, that's what Geoff called the tyrants. He once said that we – journalists – had the power to challenge every one of them, expose them, make a real difference. That was the thing with him – he always took a stand. He said we owed it to the world, and that's the only way St Peter would give us an A-grade at the Pearly Gates. He'd have got an A-star for sure. But now he's gone and I'm still here, a D-minus at best.'

'It's not your fault.'

'Then why does it feel like it is? I can't let his death be in vain. I promised him I'd never stop fighting. But it's been five whole years and what have I achieved?'

Sure, he'd travelled the world, shed light on every injustice he could. He'd won awards and gained enemies. And yet not a damn word he'd written had helped a single soul.

ELEVEN

They left the roads and joined a country trail. Even with Dylan's support, Mika winced with every step.

'This is a good place to rest for a second,' Mika said. 'Look.'

Two pillars of red-stained wood rose out of the wet grass. A curved wooden double lintel atop. It reminded Dylan of a delicate timber version of Stonehenge. Sunlight from the horizon skimmed its surface.

'That's a torii,' Mika said. 'A gateway to a Shinto shrine. You see those lion dogs?'

At the foot of the shrine, on either side of the stone path, two statues faced each other. Mischievous-looking creatures, one open-mouthed, the other tight-lipped.

'Those are the Komainu. They ward off evil spirits.'

The shrine beyond was a sturdy red timber pagoda with a steeply pitched roof, echoing the gate's design. Surrounding it were trees whose early-spring cherry blossom had somehow survived the water. The whole site exuded a majesty of both the ancient and the new.

'I wonder how many disasters this place has survived,' Dylan said.

Mika bowed to the torii and limped over the threshold.

'I won't be long. I want to pray for Itsumi,' she said, and then faced Dylan. 'And Geoff.'

'I'll come.'

'Wait. Before you enter, you must bow to the guardian deities and ask for permission to enter. Once in, don't walk in the middle of the path – that's reserved for the guardian deities. Copy me.'

He did as she said and joined her by a pavilion sheltering a water basin.

'This is the chōzubachi. Here, we purify ourselves before we proceed.' She gestured to a large ladle. 'And this is the hishaku. Hold it in your right hand and fill it with water.'

Dylan did as instructed, and filled the receptacle to the brim.

'It's symbolic,' Mika said. 'There's no need to actually wash yourself. Just pour some into your left hand, then your right. Then with your left hand wet your lips. But don't drink.'

With the water drying on his lips, Dylan followed Mika to the shrine.

'This is the haiden, the worship hall. Do you have any yen?'

Dylan pulled out his wallet. 'All I've got is a Visa card, a driver's licence and a press ID.'

'We'll come back and make an offering later.'

Mika rested her hand on a rope hanging from the roof and shook it. Chimes rang out and wet blossom fell as she bowed and mouthed words.

'There's a Japanese saying,' she said. 'Wake from death and return to life.' A tear rolled past her smile. 'I used to visit this place with my papa.'

'Where is he now?'

'We lost touch after my parents divorced.' She wiped her hands on her jeans. 'He used to love this place. He said there was something special about the blossom. He was a doctor, but he believed this was the only real place of healing.' She blinked at the sky. 'Let's return to life and travel someplace else. Dylan, tell me about England. Do they have earthquakes there?'

'I don't think so. I only really know London. It's big, busy and noisy. You don't want to go there. You want to go where the sun shines.'

'Are there any Japanese people in London?'

'Yeah, of course.'

'Then let me think of England … the Queen, fish and chips, English tea. And the music.' She moved her hips and sang as the last twinkling of dusk painted white diamonds in her eyes. 'Now sing with me,' she said and launched into another song that sounded oddly familiar despite the Japanese words.

'What is that?' he said, trying to place it.

'Come on, you *must* know it.' She repeated the words, this time exaggerating the melody.

The penny dropped. It was the Beatles. 'Ah, righto, Ringo. One more time.'

He mimicked her, his first lesson in Japanese. And as he did so, her energy bathed him, cleansing him of the world's dirtiest hour.

TWELVE

Tomioka's school was a modern high-rise with a peaked steel roof. The structure was clad in masonry and metal, built to withstand the rushes of God's own army.

'You were right to tell people to come here,' Dylan said. 'It had a better chance of surviving than anywhere else.'

Still, the water dragon had left scars. The exterior walls were stained and many of the windows had blown out. But the tide had stopped short of the top floor.

Mika urged Dylan to approach the entrance. He walked ahead and rattled the door. It wouldn't budge.

'This shouldn't be locked, right?'

She shook her head. 'It's always open, in case of an emergency.'

'I wonder why it's locked. It would have condemned any late-comers to death.'

Mika yelled out. No one answered.

'I'm going in through the window,' Dylan said. He picked up a length of timber and smashed out the shards from the window frame, then vaulted into the gloomy interior. 'Stay here.'

'But—'

A muffled *shush* came from above. Dylan put a finger to his lips. 'Did you hear that?'

He looked towards the stairwell and stole one last glance at Mika.

A new quarter moon had arrived over her shoulder, casting a murky light on the filthy stairs. He crept up, feeling every bit the intruder.

'Hello?' His voice echoed up the dripping, concrete void.

A sound whose source he couldn't identify came from above.

He arrived on the first floor. Tungsten moon beams illuminated a large open-plan room, and Dylan held his breath and tuned in.

A bird launched itself through an open window.

Shit.

The flapping faded, but the whispering ghost remained.

The room was fitted with Bunsen burners, sinks and workbenches. Smudged, ripped posters depicting the precipitation cycle and the anatomy of volcanoes took up most of the walls.

The sound grew stronger with each step. A fizzing or hissing.

The stench of rotten egg hit the back of his throat.

He tracked the noise to the back wall and a bench with four gas valves.

Three of the tap handles pointed down. One was up.

Open.

He touched the lever, intending to shut it off, and felt a sharp pressure against his neck.

Someone was holding a knife to his throat.

THIRTEEN

Every synapse told him to run, but the warm, sour breath of the phantom at his shoulder told Dylan that wasn't an option. The thin edge of the blade pressed against his windpipe, and a hand gripped his hair and yanked it back, exposing his neck.

'Wait! I'm a reporter. You can't do this.'

'Eigo Kankōkyaku ... Hijō ni subarashī.'

'I don't speak Japanese! Please, stop!'

The room narrowed. Time seemed to slow. Dylan conjured the only Japanese he knew, as foolish as it seemed under the circumstances, and began to whisper the song Mika had taught him. His voice cracked as the words tumbled from his mouth.

'Nantekotta!'

The shadow laughed, a high-pitched taunt. A blow to the back of his leg sent Dylan to his knees, and the knife pressed hard into his neck.

The memories came, crowding him now. Iraq, blows to his head, a gun in his face, the heat, sweat, flies, shouting, starvation.

Geoff.

The slice was slow. The edge of the scalpel sharp. Warm blood trickled down his neck.

A scream came from beyond the room.

The cutting paused.

Another man's voice boomed into the room.

His killer shouted towards the stairwell, snapping Dylan back to the moment.

If he was going to die, he could at least see their face.

He grabbed the phantom's arm, dragged it downward and launched a fist into the dark. The impact was jarring.

The knife fell to the floor.

Dylan seized it.

FOURTEEN

The phantom stood, rubbed his jaw and growled.

Dylan lunged but the blade found open air. His opponent was quick.

They stalked each other in the silver light, face to face, matching each other step for step. The moon lit up the phantom – his prison uniform, mop-top hair, jet-black eyes.

Dylan slowed, and stiffened his grip on the knife.

Jushin Okada.

Headlines and standfirsts flashed through Dylan's mind. Known internationally as the Merchant of Fukushima, Okada was number two in the ranks of the Notorious Three. The world's most infamous extortionist. The Fortune 500's blackmailing bogeyman. The monster under every politician's bed. Disciple of the Tomioka Torturer. This man had cut his teeth as an assassin.

'Sā, iki-mashō!'

'I don't know what you're saying but praying isn't going to help either of us.'

Okada grinned.

'Don't make me do this!'

The knife glinted, but Dylan's courage to use it had diminished. He had to get out.

Okada spoke in a low monotone, his words slow, rhythmic, hypnotic. He moved with quick irregular steps and half-lunges, and backed Dylan into a corner.

Another scream came from beyond the room.

The assassin glanced towards it.

Dylan tackled the man. Okada crashed to the floor on his back. Dylan held the knife to his throat, blade trembling.

'I'm leaving … I'm backing away now, and you're going to stay right there, okay?'

The light pouring through the near window vanished, a roar of laughter boomed over Dylan's head and shadow fell over him.

It's massive outline was unmistakable.

Freddie Yoka.

Dylan turned. The signature tattoos chased over his fists and arms, and converged at the top of his head. News media photographs hadn't done justice to his sheer mass. Six foot nine and north of three hundred pounds.

And one enormous hand was locked around Mika's slender neck.

The other was flat against her mouth. She screamed through his suffocating paw, tears twinkling on her cheeks.

Dylan pressed the tip of the blade against Okada's throat. 'I'll kill him! Let her go or it's game over, I swear.'

The skin broke, and blood beaded on the assassin's neck.

Yoka uncovered Mika's mouth and doubled his leverage on her neck.

'I said, let her go,' Dylan hissed.

Mika thrashed and kicked and clawed, but the giant lifted her effortlessly off her feet. Her pleading eyes flashed with terror and her tongue swelled through pale lips. Then she slumped and hung limp in Yoka's arms.

'Mika!'

Dylan sprang to his feet and plunged the knife into Yoka's stomach. The giant didn't flinch, just smacked Dylan aside.

Dylan's head started to pound, and the smell from the noxious gas escaping from the valve felt toxic.

And then he had an idea.

He reached into his pocket.

'If she's going to die, we're all going with her.'

He flicked the Zippo's lid, ran his thumb over the coarse wheel, and tossed the lighter towards the open gas tap.

FIFTEEN

A wall of yellow and orange flooded the room as a jet of flame hit the ceiling with a roar.

The back of Yoka's turquoise prison fatigues ignited, and he dropped Mika and fell to the ground, beating at the column of flames licking his torso. The hilt of the knife protruding from his abdomen began to burn, and he rolled onto his back, screaming.

Dylan jumped up and lurched through the black smoke pouring off the giant until he found Mika's limp body. He lifted her onto his shoulders as Okada tried to stamp out the fire engulfing his screaming friend. Yoka's hand spasmed and grabbed the hot knife from his charred flesh. He sat up and fixed Dylan with a murderous glare.

Dylan stumbled towards the exit amid the stench of Yoka's burnt flesh and nylon overalls, and descended the punishing stairs. He kicked open the bolted door and ran into the inky night.

Only when he'd reached the school playing field did he stop. Gasping for breath, he glanced back at the school and lay Mika on the ground. There was no trace of breath on her lips, no movement in her chest. He checked her pulse and patted her face.

'Please don't go, Mika. Please don't die.'

SIXTEEN

In the war room of *Topic International Magazine*'s Soho headquarters, Sam MacLaine lit a menthol cigarette and dialled Dylan's mobile number for the tenth time.

'Come on.'

She exhaled a plume of smoke across a table littered with coffee cups, notepads and laptops, and surrounded by journalists, personal assistants and staff writers.

No answer. Damn the man.

Paul, one of the journalists – whose hair matched his signature white linen suit – raised his hand.

'Ma'am, might it be possible that Dylan is, in fact, dead? Terrible things, quakes and tsunamis, you know. I remember those awful scenes in Kashmir back in—'

'If he's dead, he's fired,' Sam said.

She dialled again while beating out the orange glow of her largely unsmoked cigarette in the bottom of a small glass bowl. Still nothing. She grunted, tossed her mobile into the middle of the desk, and took a sip of her coffee.

'Cold.' She held the mug in the air.

Nineteen-year-old Violet sprang to her feet. 'I'm so sorry, Sam. I'll make sure to steam the milk twice in future—'

'Less words, hotter coffee. Okay, everybody, let's assume Dylan's dead. Now what? We've lost our boots-on-the-ground eye-witness account on this huge international breaking story that every news outlet in the world is just jizzing in people's faces. And guess what? The people are lapping it up. *Lapping it up*. It's already 10 a.m. and what do my highly paid crack team of journalists have for me?' She held up a few pieces of paper. 'A fluff piece on history's biggest earthquakes. No offence, Paul, but Violet could do a better job than this shit – even when she's having one of her secret cries in the stationery cupboard.'

Violet blushed. 'Thank you, Sam. Thank you—'

'Fuck off,' Sam said, and threw the report at Violet. 'I don't need fluff. I need *jizz*. Where's my jizz?' She lit another cigarette. 'And may I remind you all that if Dylan is dead, I've also lost the six-page Notorious Three piece that was holding together the next issue. All I have now are blank pages and staples. You've brought me exactly zero stories of substance for next month. And I need content for the website an hour ago. So, people, suggestions.'

The faces around the table looked at each other.

Kasper, her youngest reporter, played with the collar of his polo shirt then lifted his other hand tentatively. He cleared his throat, and said, 'If Dylan's not picking up his mobile then, er, maybe we could try reaching him at his hotel?'

Now there was an idea. The boy could do with some field experience.

SEVENTEEN

Dylan lifted Mika's lids. Her eyes were vacant, dead. He started chest compressions, counted to thirty, pinched her nose and breathed into her mouth.

'Come on, Mika.'

He pressed on her chest again, every push leaving him weaker. Fine grit and dirt stained the skin on his arms, while Mika, pale in the moonlight, looked oddly graceful, at peace. He leant in again, his lips grazing hers, and felt her breath on his skin.

Thank God.

She coughed, and he helped her sit. Then she stood, legs unsteady, and ran a trembling hand through her scorched hair.

'What happened?'

'You're okay. We got away, that's all that matters. We need to go.'

'Who were they?' she said, and limped a few steps.

'Don't worry about that. Just focus on getting back to the recon point where the soldiers are. Can you walk?'

She stopped and gawped at his neck. 'Your throat's smeared with blood. What happened? Tell me who they were.'

'The smaller guy was Jushin Okada, second in command of the Notorious Three, best known for his extortion racket. The fat man was the so-called Artist. His real name is Freddie Yoka. He's a sadistic pervert, and a drug procurement and distribution superpower.' Dylan glanced over his shoulder. 'He's also the head of a sex-trafficking ring. He kidnaps and drugs women, then controls them through addiction. And if they don't play along, they get sent back to the Torturer.'

'Why Artist?'

'Tabloid humour. He tattoos his victims with his tag – a blue wolf. It's like a brand. Once a woman has that tag on her body, she belongs to him, and she'll be shipped across the world to a network of private islands. The only way to leave his employ is to buy your freedom for 100,000 US dollars. Cash. The joke is, his slaves don't get paid so a buyout is impossible.'

'Private islands?'

'They're hooked up with spy cameras and audio gear. The Three invite powerful people, entangle them with one of the women and record it. The footage is used to extort money or manipulate scientific reports and political decisions.'

Mika seemed to phase out for a moment. Then she said, 'Where were the children?'

'I didn't see anyone apart from those two guys. I'm sorry.'

She slumped to her knees, and Dylan grabbed her.

'Let's not leap to conclusions. Maintain hope. We don't know anything for sure. Well, we know one thing – we were lucky to get out alive. It's a good job their boss wasn't around.'

'The Tomioka Torturer,' she whispered.

'Yeah, Shinsuke Takahashi. The worst of the Three, from what I've heard.'

'I don't want to know.'

'He has a fetish for watching his victims suffer. Sometimes he hooks a car battery up to their genitals. When they fall asleep, he electrocutes them. He also likes to extract fingernails. For those who don't behave, he cuts off body parts – one a day. Could be a finger, a hand, a leg. Then he makes them watch their dismembered body parts being—'

'I said I don't want to know.'

Dylan apologised for rambling, then summoned the memory of

Shinsuke Takahashi trapped under the steel girder.
  He'd got his.
  And Dylan had never been gladder.

EIGHTEEN

Mika's fire had vanished, and this time they didn't hold hands. She muttered quietly about the poor children and their parents while Dylan struggled to navigate the once tranquil village.

Hundreds had likely been dragged along by the tide and swept into the sea. The thought haunted Dylan and he stopped.

'I need to get out of here,' he said.

'I'm going home,' Mika said, and limped forward.

'You can't, Mika. Your home doesn't exist anymore.'

She shook her head and continued on.

'Stop!' he said. 'Please. We're both exhausted and there's nothing here for either of us. It's been the world's shittiest day, and I'm heartbroken for you, for everyone. I'm going to Tokyo – the magazine has a marketing agent there. I can contact the office and get a report to them. You should come with me.'

The moon lit the tears on Mika's face. She shook her head.

The recon point was empty. Gone were the residents and the soldiers, leaving in their wake a dreadful quiet.

Mika called out into the night. No response.

Dylan felt a sudden and desperate need for sleep. If they hadn't gone to the school they'd have been be out of here by now. He found his phone in a puddle, still dead, and stared at the spiderweb cracks on the screen. A familiar splintering in his mind rendered him unable to think for a moment.

Mika sat on the mast of a small sailboat that lay on its side, pulled off her shoe and massaged her swollen ankle.

'I'm going to my mom's in Cape Sōya.'

'Is that south, anywhere near Tokyo?'

'It's as far north as you can go.'

Tiny flecks of snow fell from the sky, dusting the earth like ash. Dylan pitched his phone high into the air.

'It makes more sense to go to Tokyo.'

'I'm going to stay with my mom.'

'In that case, I guess this is goodbye.' He tucked his dirty white shirt into his waistband. 'I'm sorry—'

'You're not.'

'Excuse me?'

'You have your story. Congratulations. Now go. Enjoy your trip home. Say hi to your editor for me.' She turned away.

'I have a job to do.'

'Then go do it.'

'You wouldn't understand. You're just a schoolteacher.'

'Listen to yourself, Mr Journalist. So arrogant. So busy chasing a story that you've missed the most important thing of all – that so many people died today. But you're just a self-interested know-it-all trying to please a ghost. So go! I'm staying here till the morning. Then I'll figure a way out on my own. Goodbye.' She put her shoe on and staggered ahead.

'Mika, don't—'

She froze.

Ahead was a newly planted notice board. She stood at it, open-mouthed.

'What does it say?'

'Japan Ground Self-Defence Force – North Eastern Field Army Nuclear Emergency Alert. March 11, 2011. Instructions to all persons. Evacuate this area immediately. All people within twenty kilometres of the Fukushima 1 nuclear power plant in Ōkuma must evacuate. Please report to the nearest emergency centre if you require assistance. An incident has been reported. There has been NO abnormal release of radioactivity from the station at this time. Emergency staff are responding to the situation. Locations and survival information has been sent to all mobile devices. Tune in to local media for further information. If you are reading this notice, you must evacuate immediately.'

Dylan suddenly felt a hundred years old.

NINETEEN

Kasper Ronnie sat in an undersized plastic chair that might possibly have been designed for a child. He fidgeted with his glasses and tried not to wilt under Sam's penetrating gaze.

'But why me? Anyone could go. Send Violet,' he said.

'Violet is practically a schoolgirl. She can barely make coffee. Do you advocate dispatching a child, a useless one at that, to a disaster area?'

'That's exactly my point! It's a catastrophe over there. The very thing we should *not* be doing is flying someone directly into it.'

Sam lent back and hit Kasper with a carbon-steel glare. The clock ticked as smoke spiralled from her cigarette. Kasper melted deeper into his seat.

She slammed her hand down on the desk. 'You're in the news game now. Most people would kill for this opportunity. What if Bob Woodward and Carl Bernstein had your attitude? This is what we do. We go out there and we get the story. We sacrifice! And don't worry, my insurance will cover any mishaps.'

'What do you mean, mishaps?'

'In case you die.' Her cigarette hand flopped. 'You think I'd assign an uninsured journalist to a catastrophe? I've been in this business too long. I promise you, Kasper, I'll cover the bill for your modest funeral. You can die knowing your horrible death boosted circulation.'

'You're insane.'

'This is what it takes.' She checked her nails.

'I quit.'

'Quitters have a hard time finding work in this industry. You think *The Guardian* wants to hire a pussy? You assume *The Times* will pay you to hide under your desk? Look, if you go to Tomioka you might die, which FYI, is highly, highly unlikely. Sure, you might piss your pants, but you won't be the first reporter to leave the comfort of their computer and do some actual work. And when you come back here, you'll be a household name – to hardcore fans of alternative journalism, at least. This could make your career. Imagine. Kasper Ronnie, award-winning international adventurer and scooper of stories. The man who saved a magazine. Even better, the man who went to the rescue of the one and only Dylan Solly. Sound good?'

Kasper couldn't help it. He cracked a smile.

Sam opened a drawer, produced a plane ticket and threw it at him.

'Pack up your laptop. The taxi's waiting outside.'

TWENTY

Dylan stared at the sign's unfathomable kanji characters. The epicentre of a nuclear emergency. It seemed unreal. He tried to speak but nothing came out of his mouth. Mika sat on the ground and looked up at the moon. Dylan hunkered down next to her.

'I guess it's about midnight,' he said. 'No way to know for sure.'

Mika planted her chin on her fist. 'I wonder how many times over the course of my life I'll relive this night, how many mornings it'll be behind my eyes when I wake.'

The town was a cemetery, the derelict buildings its tombstones. Garbage surrounded them. But it was the stillness that struck him. No nocturnal creatures, no sound, not even a breeze. It was exactly how he imagined hell – not a scorched fiery inferno but a gloomy, endless vale of despair.

'So where's the nearest emergency station that sign mentioned?'

'There.' Mika pointed to a single-storey building with no roof, no windows and only three walls.

'And the nuclear plant?'

'About ten or twelve kilometres away.' She slipped off her shoe and again massaged a foot that had turned various shades of purple.

'So what's that, about a two-hour walk?'

With Mika's ankle, the journey would be hard enough, never mind navigating the glass, wood and metal debris in the dark.

He recalled her earlier words. Was he really that selfish?

'You won't make it anywhere on your own with that ankle,' he said. 'We need a car.'

'Good luck.'

'I think our luck ran out this morning.'

A smile twitched on her face. 'Yep.'

He bit his thumbnail. 'That was pretty bad back there, wasn't it?' She nodded.

'And you're right, by the way. I'm a conceited arsehole.'

'Yeah, but you saved me, so it's okay.'

A handprint-shaped bruise now marked Mika's neck, and the tips of Yoka's thumbs had left deep blue marks either side of her spine.

'And going to your mother's isn't a bad idea,' he said. 'I'll help you get there. Then I'll head to Tokyo.'

'I'll manage on my own.' Mika drew her fringe in front of her eyes and inspected the burnt ends.

Dylan took a breath. 'I doubt that. Plus, I want to help. The magazine can wait.'

'You've changed your tune.'

'How far is Cape Sōya?'

'Approximately 1,500 kilometres.'

'Ouch. We definitely need a car.'

A hundred feet or so in front of them, a red haulage truck lay on its side, buried under a mass of bricks. Moonlight reflected off its smashed headlights.

Mika slumped. 'I'm tired and hungry, my hair's burnt and my foot hurts. What are we going to do?'

Dylan scratched his new stubble. 'My rented Mazda will be long gone by now, probably buried like that lorry or swept away. We've no chance of finding anything drivable around here. Our only option appears to be a piggyback. I'll let you carry me first.'

'Wow! Englishmen are so gracious. I thought that was just a stereotype.'

'Okay, let's park the piggyback idea. Ever seen the movie *Up*? We could try that thing with the balloons—'

Mika grabbed Dylan's arm.

'It was a joke. I—'

'My apartment!' she said. 'It has a secure ground-floor parking lot. My car might be there.'

Maybe. At least it sounded more promising than balloons.

TWENTY-ONE

Mika and Dylan stood at the foot of her ruined apartment block. He shivered. It was a carcass. He scurried to the rear, Mika limping behind. They entered the garage through a large, jagged hole in the breezeblock wall. Moonlight crept along the floor but stopped short of the far corner, where cars were piled as high as the ceiling. A few feet away, a row of vehicles lay on their sides. Elsewhere, a lucky few were battered but still on their tyres.

'It looks like the school's collection of Tomica cars after recess,' Mika said.

'I'm not sure if any vehicle could have survived this.'

Mika shrugged. 'We did. Why can't a car?'

'Which one's yours?'

'I can't see it. It's too dark. One second.'

She patted her pockets. 'Oh.'

Dylan rubbed his eyes. 'Nobody ever says "Oh" when it's good news.'

'I think I lost— No, wait …'

She rummaged in her jeans, held up the fob with an expression of pure victory, and pressed it.

The yellow blink that lit up the lot was nothing short of beautiful.

They located the vehicle – a Suzuki Jimny – which lay on its side.

'At least it's not piled in that corner,' Dylan said. 'Let's see what I can do with it.'

He laid his palms on the tiny SUV's roof and said, 'Stand back.'

'Wait for me.' Mika came alongside him. 'Ready? San, ni, ichi.'

They pushed, and a satisfying crunch echoed around the walls as the Suzuki lurched back onto four wheels.

'The exterior's in good shape, all things considered.' The wing mirror was crushed and the passenger door dented, but who cared? He peered through the window. 'Check out the interior. It's bone dry.'

Mika got inside and started the engine. It made a weird ticking noise, then died. She tried again, twice more. Then the car coughed and spluttered, and settled on an irregular, low-powered purr. She clapped her hands and patted the steering wheel.

'That's my lady!'

'I was so sure it wouldn't start,' Dylan said.

'So rude.'

She turned the heating up and flicked on the headlights. The broad beam illuminated the broken wall and the pile of cars.

'This is a miracle,' Dylan said, fighting with the jammed passenger-side door. It wouldn't budge, so he climbed through the window.

Mika tapped the accelerator and winced. 'My ankle. I can't do it.'

Dylan braced his legs against the jammed door. It sprang open and he got out and walked around to the driver's side. 'Move over.'

Mika shuffled into the passenger seat and began to click her fingers and sway her torso. Her energy was contagious and Dylan couldn't help but laugh.

They drove out of the parking lot and over the uneven ground until they found clear open road. The headlights spotlit the damage that Tomioka had been dealt, and Dylan's smile withered.

He stopped the car and turned to Mika. 'Where are we going and how the hell do we get there?'

'Head north to Hokkaido,' Mika said, and tapped the dash-mounted TomTom.

'Eighteen hours? We can't do that in one go. Let's get a safe distance and rest – God knows we need it. In the meantime, let's see what the radio has for us.'

He'd never wanted to hear the news so bad. The dash clock read 7 p.m. Was that right? Could that really only be the time?

Mika tuned in to a news bulletin and translated. Over 8,000 had been killed in the tsunami. Hundreds of bodies had washed up on Sendai Beach. There was concern over the whereabouts of the Notorious Three. Government officials were monitoring three nuclear sites. Onagawa was stable – a fourteen-metre seawall had prevented flooding. The Fukushima Daini nuclear site in Tomioka had flooded but was also holding. The power plant had been shut down as a protection measure.

She paused, then continued, her words a stutter now.

'The Daiichi power plant in Ōkuma ... suffered severe damage. Emergency generators that cool the reactor core offline ... Fuel rods exposed ... Japan on high alert for possible meltdown ... Tens of thousands evacuated ... Stock market in crisis ... Oh my God, Dylan ... Analysts say a full nuclear disaster's possible within hours.'

She lowered the volume and stared out of the window.

Dylan drove. What else could he do?

TWENTY-TWO

Dylan felt lost in time, as if they were caught in a loop. Black tarmac. White lines. Darkness in the rear view. Uncertainty ahead.

West of Tomioka, they passed a forty-foot fishing vessel beached on the roadside, its captain and crew long gone, the masthead and bridge caved in.

Otherwise, the district hadn't suffered the same level of destruction as the coastal part of town, not from the wave at least. Not that the earthquake hadn't left its mark. Some of the older homes had been flattened, others shaken, leaving rooftops cantilevering. The main road had snapped down the centre line as far as he could see, and he slowed the SUV.

'It's a ghost town,' he said.

Restaurant tables with chopsticks, condiments, food and drinks had been abandoned. Clothes wrapped in plastic, waiting to be collected, were piled outside a dry cleaner's. A fully-stocked store's doors were open but the lights were out.

Those who'd frequented this once thriving boulevard had seemingly bolted in an instant.

'It feels haunted,' Mika said. 'I can't process it.'

The radio informed them that National Route 6 couldn't be accessed, so they approached the Jōban Expressway, a carriage way that snaked up the coast and led to Sendai.

Mika emptied the storage compartment in the passenger door, checked the glove box, then lifted Dylan's elbow off the centre console.

'Yes!' she said, and held up a small pink bag.

'What is it?'

'Puccho. It's strawberry candy. Chewy.'

She unwrapped some and placed them in Dylan's hand.

'You should sleep,' he said. 'I'll wake you if we stop anywhere.'

'Maybe later.'

He looked at the bruises on her throat. 'How's your neck?'

She smiled. 'You know, neck-y.'

He focused on the road ahead, but let his mind wander – thinking about Mika's grace, her smile, her hair, every curve and every shadow on her face. But within seconds the events of the day intruded. The shaking, the flood, the wet ground, the chaos. And the Tomioka Torturer reaching out for help, trapped, dying in front of him.

Perhaps something good had come out of today. The Notorious Three had become two. It was the barest of threads in a silver lining.

And he had an article to write. Thank God he'd never have to meet those people again. Just this trip north, then back to normality. Headlines, photographs, word counts, fonts, opening lines, concluding thoughts, and how his own experience would radically change the narrative.

The ethics of his decision to sentence Shinsuke Takahashi to death were troubling. Would he include it or omit it?

The smooth purr of tyre rubber on tarmac gave way to a high-pitched whine. There was a thud, the Suzuki shuddered, and steam billowed out from the bonnet and engulfed the windows.

Dylan slammed on the brakes and tapped the steering wheel. 'Know anything about cars?'

TWENTY-THREE

Mika shook her head and rubbed her eyes. 'Should we pop the hood and look inside?'

'I've no idea what I'd be looking for.'

The vapour cloud misted over the headlights. They stayed put. A minute or so later, Mika broke the silence.

'That was the first time I've ever been scared of the Three.'

'Really? You spent your whole life in Tomioka and were never concerned for your safety, not even once? You know all the stories, right?'

She chewed her candy for a moment, then said, 'I heard. How could I avoid it? Even the children at school talk about it. I think the steam's clearing. Let's give it a minute. Maybe we just need to top up the water.'

'Don't change the subject. Indulge me. You were honestly never scared? Not even when those bodies were found in the woodland a few years back?'

'No.'

'How come? I'd like to know. It might make an interesting angle for—'

'Do you always have to pursue a story? We're stuck on this road. What are we going to do about the car?'

'We're safe. We've come far enough. And we can sleep in here if we need to.' Dylan switched off the engine. 'Anyway, what's wrong with chasing a story? There are worse habits. Look, I know it's kind of annoying but all we are is a collection of tall tales. And I'm curious. My readers will be too. Because most people in Tomioka seem terrified. Just look at the numbers. The population declined year on year – more people uprooting their lives so they could get away from it all. But you stayed and lived happily in that town.'

'I didn't say I was happy.'

'What does that mean?'

'We should get water for the engine or—'

'You didn't answer my question.'

'Stop!'

The constant questions, his badgering. It was worse than a courtroom cross-examination. She got out and limped across the road towards the grass.

'Where are you going?' Dylan called out.

Then he was beside her, and she couldn't hold it inside any longer.

'I'm sick of this. Sick of your obsessing over a scoop that you can take back home like a trophy. Don't you ever turn it off?'

'No. Why would I? What else is there?' He threw his arms in the air. 'What else am I supposed to be? What else is there to care about? Friends? I don't have any. Family? Haven't seen them in a decade. If I don't write, no one gives a shit if I exist. You think the readers care that I'm thirty-three and live in a bedsit by myself? That the closest thing I have to a friend is my editor? Writing is all I have. So since you seem to have all this shit figured out, tell me – what else is there?'

'What about the *people* in the story? But who cares, right? As long as you hit your word count.'

She walked on, trundling over plants and shrubs until she reached a wooden fence. It was short and she could have stepped over it if not for her bad ankle, so she walked around to the gate.

Ahead was a house with a steep roof and deep eaves. On the wooden veranda, a single candle burned. Small creatures orbited the orange flame, and she could hear the delicate chirrup of crickets from the reeds at the side the house. The sound was natural, reassuring.

She listened for a moment, then knocked on the front door. A swallow in flight was carved deep in the dark-oak grain. Small red and green windows lay in a square around it. A shadow beyond the glass moved, then the door opened and an elderly man in a collarless cotton shirt stroked his trimmed silver beard and bowed.

'I'm sorry to disturb you,' she said, bowing too. 'I know it's late, but I'm desperate and my car—'

The man nodded and beckoned her inside. Dylan came up behind her, breathing hard. The man waved Dylan in.

She introduced them. The man smiled, and spoke in Japanese. 'You're the schoolteacher from the city. I remember your picture in the newspaper.' He took her hand. 'I'm sorry for your loss. It was so terrible. Please, come in. It's an honour to welcome you into my home.'

'What did he say?' Dylan asked.

'Nothing,' she said.

Not that. Not yet.

TWENTY-FOUR

'My name is Nao.' He bowed again. 'And that's Yoshi.' He pointed to an elderly tabby by the fire.

Mika didn't translate for Dylan. Didn't want to.

Dylan just nodded. 'Ah, yes, a lovely cat.'

She continued to speak in Japanese, thanking Nao for taking them in and complimenting him on his home.

'It's been a long time since I've had company,' Nao said. 'It's nice to share the place for a change. You see this?' He gestured to a picture on the wall, a hand-drawn blueprint of the house. 'Fifty-five years ago, my wife and I built this house with our own hands.'

The space felt settled, loved.

'When you build a home, you construct a life,' Nao said, 'so design it well. That's what my wife used to say.' He looked between Dylan and Mika. 'Problems?'

She shook her head. 'A pointless argument.'

'I mean with your car.'

'Ah, it broke down. Something's wrong with the engine.'

'I'm sure we can fix it. Everything can be fixed. But it's too dark now. Rest here tonight. You're both welcome to stay.' He lifted a finger and said, in his best English, 'Tea!'

'Please,' Mika said, grateful for the offer.

'Very kind,' Dylan said. 'And thank you for taking us in.'

Nao invited them to sit and headed for the kitchen.

The house looked like something Mika had once clipped out of a glossy magazine and attached to her 2004 dream board – minimalist with triple-height ceilings, clean lines and natural wood, all lit by candles and warmed by an open stove. Heavy black pine rafters had intersected slender beams that reached up from a tatami floor, the kind a family dog would surely have left paw prints on after wet walks. She'd imagined towelling off the pup's legs, staging the corners of the room with plants, their graceful leaves complementing the colour of the walls. At the back, Shoji doors had led to a garden where a modest waterfall fed a small stone bath she'd dreamed of soaking in on lazy Sundays.

But the dream board had long gone, and the vision vanished. None of it was possible after Hiro had been murdered.

Dylan sat by Mika on a zabuton floor cushion in front of the fire. His hands were filthy, his clothes covered in fine grit. He stared at his scuffed, grey palms and whispered, 'I'm sorry, Mika. I just can't turn it off.'

'This is a minka house,' she said. 'A pre-war hand-crafted home you find in rural areas of Japan. I always wanted to live in a place like this.'

Nao returned with a tray and sat on a cotton pillow. They took tea and warmed themselves by the blazing stove. Nao and Mika exchanged words, then she turned to Dylan.

'Nao's asking if you want some food.'

'Yes, I'm absolutely starving. Thank you.'

Nao left with a bow, and Dylan toyed with the chain around his neck. Here he was again, as broken down as the Suzuki and an honest-to-God burden.

'This is Yoshi,' Mika said, stroking the old cat. 'I love that name.'

Nao returned with a cucumber and sesame salad, three bowls and some water, then sat and placed his palms in front of his chest. Mika did the same.

'Itadakimasu.'

The old man and Mika shared words, and from their tone, Dylan assumed they were about the day's events. He left them to it and focused instead on the meal and the respite it offered, albeit temporary.

The uncomfortable memory fog receded as Nao spoke gently of easier times and topics. Mika began translating for Dylan.

'Nao asked if you say grace in your culture. He says he's seen it on TV and that you're welcome to do so if you do that kind of thing.'

Nao offered a wise, kindly grin.

'I don't normally,' Dylan said, 'though technically I'm a Methodist, and it does feels like a time to show gratitude. So if you'll allow me ...' He bowed his head. 'Be present at our table, Lord. Be here and everywhere adored. These mercies bless and grant that we may feast in fellowship with Thee. Amen.'

'Now, it's my turn ...' Mika said. 'I know, let's do what the school children do at mealtimes. I'll give you the English version.'

She started clapping and began to sing. Nao joined in. 'Lunch, lunch, I'm happy! Hands have been washed. Eat everything! Chew well. All together we give thanks. Thank you for this food. Please. Start. Eating!'

Mika picked up her chopsticks, but her appetite had dissolved. She'd never teach that class again, never see those young faces smile, frown, grow older. The community was dead.

The log fire cracked, spitting bright orange flecks. Mika looked down at her hands.

'Those poor children ... we must be the only three people for miles. Nao, how come you're still here? Everyone else has evacuated because the nuclear plant's been damaged.'

He smiled and nodded towards the cat. 'I'm the same as Yoshi. Too old and set in my ways to move.'

'You should come with us. We're going to Cape Sōya, but we can drop you anywhere along the way.'

'For fifty-five years I've been here, living the life that I built with my wife. She's gone now, but her spirit's in this place. My home is who I am.'

'But the whole town has been told to evacuate. It's too dangerous to stay,' Mika said.

'I heard. It's such a terrible shame. Everything's in danger for as far as the eye can see, and beyond – humans, animals, all life.'

'So why stay?'

'Who will feed my cat?' He stroked the tabby. 'I could take Yoshi with me, but so many left in a panic. What if they never return? What will happen to the domesticated animals left behind? They've been abandoned. It's not fair. The animals shouldn't have to pay for our mistakes.' Nao pointed at the wall. 'Over the field is Tsutsui Farm. What happens when the farmer doesn't show up with breakfast tomorrow? Who will feed the pigs?' He took a sip of water. 'I will.'

Yoshi pushed his head into Nao's thigh and purred.

'But you might die,' Mika said.

'Some things – like your car – can be fixed with labour and know-ledge. Others require sacrifice and time. The universe will do its work, and I will do mine.'

He raised his glass and toasted the air.

TWENTY-FIVE

Nao gave Mika the guest suite, a concealed bedroom at the side of the house, and made a bed for Dylan on the living-room floor. Then, with a grin, he handed Dylan a tumbler and a full bottle of Saké.

'Arigatou,' Dylan said, in his best Japanese accent.

His right eye was more fatigued than the rest of his body, and tension was holding it to ransom – a sure sign that a migraine was coming. He held the lid closed with his cold fingers, and felt the pressure ease a little.

Nao produced a smoker's pipe, and waved Dylan into the garden. Tired, but unable to deny his host's goodwill, Dylan walked into the lemongrass-scented night and sat by the waterfall. The stone was cold, but the moon overhead and the pitter-patter of water behind him was comfort enough. Nao reclined next to a table on which a forest of bonsai had been planted in distinctive glazed pots. He pressed the tip of the pipe's long white stem to his lips, examined his miniature acreage, and blew smoke towards Dylan.

'Tabako?'

Dylan did what polite guests do – took a toke and held back a cough.

'Strong stuff,' he said.

'English?' Nao asked.

'Yeah,' Dylan said, trying not to choke.

Nao nodded in approval and pointed to Dylan's troubled eye.

'Stress, I think,' Dylan said.

Nao shuffled over to a little garden shed and came back with a cup and an artist's brush. He gestured for Dylan to close his eyes.

Dylan did as he'd asked, and as the crickets chirruped, something swept across his lid. He opened his able eye. The old man was holding a red-stained brush. He lifted the cup and said something that sounded like 'so crisp moon'. The ointment smelled like eucalyptus and eased the pressure. With that, the smoke and the Saké, he felt at peace for the first time since the quake.

Nao pointed the tip of the brush to Mika's room and smiled, as if he knew a schoolyard secret. 'Diransan to Mikasan?'

Dylan shook his head.

Nao scurried inside and returned with the framed black-and-white photograph of young Nao and a woman, presumably his wife. He sat next to Dylan and gave a thumbs-up.

Dylan smiled.

'Gone,' Nao said.

'I'm sorry to hear that.'

The old man patted his heart, then pointed again to Mika's room and nudged Dylan. Then he laughed so hard he almost fell off his perch.

The two men worshipped the night with Saké. They'd snapped together like jigsaw pieces, and the drunker they got, the better the edges fit.

'Diransan to Mikasan,' Nao said again.

He didn't let it drop for the rest of the evening.

TWENTY-SIX

Hi, Kasper Ronnie here. Welcome to my new blog, Danger Blurb, a *Topic International Magazine* web exclusive. I'm on my way to Japan – the Land of the Rising Sun, famous for sushi, karate, pornographic cartoons and the catastrophe people just can't get enough of. My mission: locate Dylan Solly, who hasn't been heard from since the morning of the quake.

This morning, I left HQ with nothing but a laptop, passport and the coffee stains on my polo shirt (such is the glamour of top-flight journalism). I'm currently in the VIP lounge at Heathrow, and as I write this from the vantage of a comfy but not overly private seat, I'm stuffing as many tiny croissants into my mouth as I can and rinsing them down with equally proportioned cups of coffee. Don't worry, readers, I've also stuffed my plastic carry-on bag with small cans of pop and the least perishable fruits.

Each day you'll follow me as I heroically enter the heart of a disaster zone without a single thought for my own personal safety. I know most people would be fearful of such an assignment, but frankly it's an honour to be chosen for the job. When the editor pitched me the idea, there wasn't a moment's hesitation in my mind. She was right to call on me because I'm the only man that can save Dylan Solly. And if any awards were to come out of this, well, c'est la vie.

Dylan's been a hero of mine for a long time – as I'm sure he's been for many of you. I've been following him ever since his awful experience as a hostage in Iraq. It's a testament to Dylan's popularity as a journalist, and as a person, that *Topic International*'s been swamped with concerned calls asking about him since news of his disappearance was leaked. Damn those leakers.

I'm sure he'd appreciate all the support you've shown by phone, social media, letter and email, and I know in my heart of hearts that Dylan would want nothing more than for all of you to follow me on Twitter.

Dylan was last heard from on the morning of the disaster(s) in Tomioka, so that's where my search begins. Ah! That's my first-class flight being announced. I better get myself to the gate. Wish me luck!

I'll post updates here, so check back tomorrow for all the latest from Japan. You can also follow me on social media: @HeroKasperRonnie.

P.S. I've posted several recent pictures of Dylan. Please check them. If you have any information about his whereabouts, have heard from him in the past few days or have any funny anecdotes about him, please hit me up on Twitter with the hashtag #SaveSolly #HeroKasper 💪 **JP** 👍 (meme cats also welcome).

TWENTY-SEVEN

Mika dreamed of malnourished bloodhounds under a shrinking English sky, then woke to the twitter of birds greeting the morning. It could only be a better day surely.

She joined Dylan in the kitchen and listened to Nao's old battery-powered Toshiba radio. The news wasn't good – the electricity was still out in most places, and the death toll was estimated at 16,000.

'It's awful,' she said. 'The earthquake was the largest on record, and villages in Sendai had just eight minutes' warning. Some areas were hit with heavy snowfall at the same time as the tsunami.'

'What about the nuclear power plant?' Dylan asked.

'They're saying the pressure's still too high in one of the reactors at Fukushima 1. The cooling system's down. Workers are going to vent some of the radioactive steam and pour in fresh water. They're discussing the possibility of an explosion when the hydrogen in the steam mixes with the oxygen.'

A throaty growl erupted outside. Mika looked through the window overlooking the road. Nao was standing in front of the Suzuki's propped-up hood. The engine ticked over, and he patted himself on the back.

'He got it running,' she said.

Nao walked into the kitchen, clutching an oily rag.

'The radiator was clogged,' he said. 'And I'm surprised any of the electronics work in that thing. The fuse box is badly water-damaged so you'll need to get it replaced, but I've done what I can and it should get you home. I told you, everything can be fixed.' He grinned. 'Wait, there's one exception. You can't fix people.'

His laughter was infectious, even to Dylan, who'd had no idea what the man had said.

Nao served grilled fish and eggs with furikake, and Mika taught Dylan a little Japanese at the breakfast table – hajimemashite, nice to meet you. It took him several attempts to get the pronunciation down, but Nao credited him for being a quick learner, even for someone so hungover.

She showered and composed a thank-you note while Nao rechecked the engine coolant levels and Dylan cleaned the dishes.

'You braided your hair,' Dylan said. 'It looks nice.'

She nodded and continued scratching on the paper.

They headed out to the car, and Nao gave her a hamper stocked with food, bottles of water and two blankets.

'For the long road ahead,' he said.

He bowed, shook Dylan's hand, and slipped him a roll of bank-notes in a manner that suggested he hadn't wanted Mika to see.

A light breeze caught the notes and Dylan chased them.

Nao shrugged and smiled at Mika. 'What shopkeepers are left to sell me anything?'

Mika wiped her eyes and stared down at the grass, misted with early dew. 'I'm leaving Tomioka for only the second time in my life. I might never be able to come back. I know I have to go but I don't want to. I just want to go home.'

'You have the power to carry on,' Nao said. 'It's not easy, but you have to persevere. You're young. You have so much of your life to live. When the time is right, you'll find a place to build a new home.' He glanced at Dylan. 'Just be sure to build it well, Mikasan. And enjoy the journey.'

'I just don't know what to expect.'

'Expectations are seldom married with truth. Just go forward and remember, no matter what happens, you must keep going and understand that it's all part of the journey.'

'It just seems like such a long way,' Mika said.

Nao held her hand. 'Trillions of years from now, the universe will stop. It'll cool and shrink into a tiny ball, and the journey will be over for everyone and everything. It's just a question of when. The journey is all we have. We must persevere.'

A rumble shook the ground. A thunderclap echoed and white vapour rose above the trees in the distance.

Nao ran to the kitchen, and returned seconds later, the radio pressed to his ear.

TWENTY-EIGHT

Kasper cleared passport control and bustled through baggage reclaim without stopping, his only worldly possessions the laptop in his hands, the phone pressed to his ear and the clothes on his back. He checked his voicemail, deleted two robo-messages about car accidents and insurance, and braced himself for Sam's typically blunt mezzo-soprano.

'Kasper meet Shultz, Shultz meet Kasper. He called the office and claimed to be a friend of Dylan's so I thought you should hook up. It won't hurt to have a tour guide. Enjoy. Bye.'

A tall, refrigerator-shaped man with bleached curly hair, Aviators and a loose white vest, held up a handwritten sign that read *Topic International – Kasper Ronnie*. Veins bulged on the surface of the man's biceps, something Kasper had only seen in action movies.

'Hey,' Kasper said. 'Er, Shultz?'

'Correct. Welcome to Japan, little fella.'

'Oh, cool, an American. Okay. Sorry, I've only just listened to Sam's message. Who are you?'

Shultz shook his head. 'Just like Dylan to not even mention his friends to his co-workers. I'll explain it to you like I explained it to your editor. I'm Dylan Solly's *best friend*. I know he's in Japan but I lost contact with him after the earthquake, and I've been worried sick. You're gonna help me locate him. Understand?' He glanced over

Kasper's shoulder. 'You alone?'

Kasper checked behind. 'I think so.'

'Good. I got a car over here. Follow me and tell me everything you know.'

TWENTY-NINE

The SUV whined at low speed, seemingly unsure of what gear it was supposed to be in, but once they hit the highway, it hummed smoothly, reassuring Dylan.

Twenty kilometres north, the scenery changed. In the fields flanking them, rows of huge solar panels glinted in the sun.

'Look at all the tech,' Dylan said. 'Fields and fields of it.'

The road narrowed, and ahead, nestled between the solar array, was a payphone.

'Stop!' Mika said, the amber light catching her dark braids. 'I want to call my mom. She'll be worried sick.'

After Mika had spoken to her mother, Dylan dialled the office, intending to let them know he was still alive and where he was headed. No one picked up so he walked back to the car.

Her seat was empty.

It was just him, the jeep, and the empty road. Where the hell was she?

'Dylan!'

He followed the sound. Mika was standing in the field, surrounded by solar panels. He ran to her.

'Let's have a picnic!' she said.

She'd rolled out one of Nao's blankets on the grass and set out food from the hamper.

'For fuck's sake, I didn't know where you were! I thought I'd gone mad, like I was having some sort of dream.'

'Maybe you are.'

'If I were in a dream, that phone call would've been much easier. The instructions were all in Japanese. I had no idea what to do.'

'It's time I started teaching you. Translating for you is boring.'

'Wow! Well—'

'No talking back to teacher. We'll start at the beginning. Repeat after me: Kon'nichiwa. Watashi Dylan Solly.'

She instructed him on how to greet strangers and introduce himself. Then came a primer on counting. Only once she was satisfied was he permitted to eat.

The rest of the class was spent lying on the blanket and looking up at the cobalt-blue sky.

'I couldn't get through to the office,' he said. 'No doubt they're busy covering the explosion.'

He still couldn't shake off the memory of it. Different from the quake. More of a pulse, a single shockwave.

Mika nodded. 'Is the world ending?'

'I don't think so. At least I hope not.'

'If it is, how would we know?' She paused. 'It might not happen in a flash. What if it's happening gradually and no one's noticed?'

Dylan shuffled on his back. The dried scab on his neck prickled in the heat.

Maybe she was right. What if it was all ending?

'Did you get through to your mum?' he said.

'She's excited about seeing me. I didn't tell her about you. She'd ask too many questions.'

'What about your dad?'

'I don't know his number.'

'That's a shame. Tell me about him.'

'I haven't seen him since my parents divorced seven years ago. When I was young, he taught me how to paint and play the harp. I'm glad I had those years. Each day, he'd meet me after school and we'd walk home hand in hand. He always wanted to know all about my classes, tutors, friends – everything. He was full of questions. And he loved American baseball and hotdogs. He was happiest on summer Sunday afternoons when we had barbecues. He was a wonderful papa. Anyway, Diransan, tell your story.'

'I don't have one.'

'Liar.'

'Fine.' He closed his eyes. 'I got this – Watashi Dylan Solly.'

'Well done.'

'I grew up in Kew, London. I'm a journalist, a successful one, thank you very much. My upbringing was easy. My father, whom I love, is a harsh and boring man. My mother makes me laugh but still treats me like I'm ten years old. My brother's determined to carry the family name back to greatness. Odd family trivia: my great-great-great-great grandfather was Lord Byron, via Ada Lovelace and the Blunt-Lytton family lines, whatever that's worth. Do you know Byron?'

She put a finger to her chin. '"In secret we met, in silence I grieve. That thy heart could forget, thy spirit deceive."'

'Nice. But I prefer, "She walks in beauty, like the night of cloudless climes and starry skies; and all that's best of dark and bright meet in her aspect and her eyes; thus mellowed to that tender light which heaven to gaudy day denies."'

Mika shook her head. '"I want a hero, an uncommon want, when every year and month sends forth a new one ..." I don't remember the rest.' She covered her mouth and giggled.

'I forget that one too. My mum's more of a Dylan Thomas fan. She used to say Byron was a radical with a wonky foot, but I think he's okay. He was a friend of the animals at least. I'm not sure why I brought him up really. I don't want people to define me via my ancestors, though people do. I can feel them weighing me against it.'

'Mr Byron, if the world's going to end – or even if it's not – you might as well be whoever you want to be.'

They took to the road again, and Mika translated the news. Again, it was all bad.

Core damage had resulted in a partial meltdown in reactor 3. An INES level-4 accident with local consequences had been declared. There were concerns about core damage to reactor 2 and talk of upgrading the incident to level 6 – a serious accident, which would make it the worst nuclear disaster since Chernobyl.

Dylan lowered the volume. 'That's enough. It reminds me of an article I wrote about the long-term psychological impact of Chernobyl on the evacuees – a 2008 winner of the Le Bell award, thank you.'

Mika mimed shooting herself in the head, but Dylan pressed on.

'Most of the folks still alive to talk about Chernobyl felt such extreme anxiety regarding the possibility of radiation exposure that they developed deep-rooted psychosomatic issues. "Radiophobia" was a word I learned on that assignment, so too the phrase "fatalistic alcoholism" – otherwise known as drinking yourself to death. These were common in those who'd fled the reactor site. Suicide and depression were frequent among the people who dealt with the stress of relocation. I hope Japan will fare better.'

'It's a country used to disasters,' Mika said. 'It sits on four tectonic plates – the Pacific Ring of Fire. Earthquakes happen every day, though they're usually small. If I remember my geography and history, Japan has a hundred and ten active volcanoes, and is the only place where nuclear bombs have ever been used in anger. From earthquakes and tsunamis in the north, to lava and mudslides in the south, it won't be easy, but we'll pull through. Like my papa once said, heating a blade makes it stronger, and grief is the fire of the soul.'

THIRTY

Welcome once more to Kasper Ronnie's heroic blog. Today, I travel to the heart of the story. This is day two of my mission, and I'm already in Japan – Tokyo to be exact. The plane landed about thirty minutes ago and, wow, first class is so comfortable. I'm still half asleep, so forgive me if I nod off— Sorry! I'm awake!

My driver, Shultz, is speeding me towards Tomioka, 'where sh*t is gonna get real' according to him. Shultz is an old friend of Dylan's, and, like many of us, has grown increasingly concerned for Mr Solly's where-abouts.

Strange fella, Shultz, to be honest. He's a gruff man from Detroit, USA, who owns the largest pickup truck I've ever seen. It's such a sight to see that it's worth the journey all by itself. Shultz doesn't talk much though, and doesn't seem to know Dylan all that well. I guess Dylan's always been a bit of an enigma to all of us. From his ordeal in Iraq and his coverage of the Kenyan post-election crisis in 2008, to the refugee crisis in Pakistan in 2009 and then tackling the Russian mob, he's told us so much about the world, yet we know so little of the man himself. This truly could be a journey of discovery – to recover the reporter, and to decipher the man.

It's warm here, but Shultz has given me a few tips on dealing with the humidity so that I can, as he puts it, 'quit my b*tch-ass whining'. Vests, white tracksuit bottoms and a drink called Pocari Sweat – a refreshing health drink that contains a balance of ions (electrolytes) and resembles the natural fluid balance in the human body. Full disclosure: thanks to the wonderful people at Pocari. They are now the official sponsor of the #SaveSolly challenge.

BREAKING NEWS. We have a lead! My editor informs me the office has received a missed call from a landline in Japan, which has been traced to a payphone 20 km outside of Tomioka. Could that be Dylan reaching out? I'm going to track down its location and learn more. Onward I go. As always, wish me luck! Tune back in tomorrow for the latest. Follow me and spread the word. @HeroKasperRonnie #HeroKasper #PocariSweat

If you have any leads or recognise Dylan from any of the photos I've been posting, hit me up on Twitter with the hashtag #SaveSolly.

P.S. I forgot to mention, there's now a reward for information – a full crate of Pocari Sweat!

THIRTY-ONE

T he road became bumpy, and Mika was bounced out of her snooze. She yawned, stretched and shielded her eyes from the bright sun. 'Where are we?'

'According to the satnav, we're crossing the Abukuma River and passing through Iwanuma. We've done about a hundred kilometres.'

She jabbed his arm. 'Let's go to Towada-Hachimantai!'

The car served as Dylan reeled from the small but painful blow. 'Calm down. Where's that? And why?'

'It's further north. It's the most beautiful place on earth. Papa took me there once. I haven't been there in years. It's the national park I told you about. There's mountains, crater lakes, a volcano, ancient forests and natural springs. We'll pass it on the way so we can stop there before we head to my mom's.'

'We're making terrible progress. We should push north and get as many miles in as we can today.'

'What's the rush? You got a big deadline? Come on, let's enjoy the journey. It's too long and boring otherwise.'

Dylan rubbed his arm. 'This park better be good.'

Mika reprogrammed the satnav as they approached Sendai – the city closest to the earthquake's epicentre in the Pacific Ocean, some seventy-two kilometres away. According to the news, Sendai's citizens had had the least warning. Within eight minutes, just as the snow had begun to fall, a wave of over 130 feet and travelling at 435 miles an hour had struck them direct. It had flooded the airport and destroyed the docks. And now the massive oil refinery was ablaze and all land-lines and cell-phone communications were jammed. The temperature was −4°. Many had died; more were missing, presumed dead.

The reports were borne out as Mika and Dylan passed the district. A fire burning up the refinery shone like Jupiter's gold and filled the sky with black smoke. Flakes of heavy white charcoal fell like snow around them.

'We were lucky, weren't we?' Mika said. 'To survive, I mean.'

Dylan nodded, mesmerised by the emergency workers − small figures in bright orange, wrapped up against the elements, battling the conditions, attacking the chaos. He felt cowardly, passing by to enjoy some nearby paradise.

He floored the accelerator, but disaster followed them up the coast-line. Broken men, women and children under a shifting Armageddon sky.

THIRTY-TWO

S am strode into the newsroom, silently cursing the computer, printer and assistant copywriter impeding her and her shopping bags. She smoothed down her hair – shorter, shinier and curlier than in the previous meeting. She'd made sure of it.

'Is that the lunch you got for us?' Paul said.

'Not unless you eat cashmere sweaters and Valentino shoes.'

He put his head in his hands. 'We need to eat. You promised us food two hours ago.'

Sam glared. 'How dare you.'

Paul held his arms up. 'Just my opinion.'

'Well your opinion offends me, *Paul*. Take it back.'

The man crumpled and muttered the appropriate apologies.

'You better be thankful that our blog numbers are up, thanks to that drivel Kasper keeps putting out, although I do need to have words with that little shit.'

She snatched a remote out of Violet's hand and flicked between news channels. Each station had their own version of a disaster high-light reel – CCTV footage of shaking buildings spliced with aerial shots of the tsunami and stills of the nuclear plant.

She sighed. 'Boy, did we ever need a good disaster.'

Violet peeked from behind her laptop. 'I've been thinking, maybe we should contact the British embassy in Japan. Perhaps they could help locate Dylan.'

'Shut up, Violet,' Sam snapped. 'It sounds so horrible when you speak.'

'Social media engagement's up since we announced Kasper's mission to rescue Dylan,' Paul said. 'I expect numbers for the print edition will be up, too.'

'And you all know what that means,' Sam replied. 'We can all eat for another week. Well done, *me*. Everybody else, *work work work*. We need to squeeze every drop of juice from this one. We have a golden egg on our lap. Squeeze the egg. Let's go people. Ideas – talk to me.'

Her stricken-faced employees glanced at each other.

'Come on!' Sam said. 'We need words on pages. What do I pay you for? Mummy wants content. Content is queen! Don't just look at me with your stupid eyes, get to it. Chop chop. I want the air to be filled with the tippy-tap of working hands on keyboards. Got it?'

The reporters bowed their heads and started typing.

'That's better,' Sam said. 'Just double down on the Dylan's-missing narrative. And, Paul, pull out Solly's old masterpieces from the archives and dust them off. Someone interview his mother. And he had a friend once, er … Well, there isn't anyone else to speak to, sad bastard. And whoever interviews Mummy, for the love of Moira Stuart, *please* make the sad old bird cry so we have something for the next cover. And where's the latest draft of Dylan's bio? And for heaven's sake, will someone please leak an obituary? That'll get 'em talking. Girl, this is fun. I tell you what, Dylan better not show up too soon. I'm having too much of a good time with this one. I can stretch this for at least a full quarter.'

'Call for you on line one, Sam,' Violet said. 'It's Kasper.'

'Violet, are you talking again? Eww. Fetch me a coffee. And stop sulking. Or should I say, stop acting so blue, Violet? Ha, classic zinger. I'll take the call in my office.'

Sam marched out, picked up the phone and banged her fist on the desk. 'Bloody Pocari Sweat, Kasper? You do understand *Topic*'s editorial policy, right? No individual sponsor gets space in an article. That applies to web content too, you dimwit.'

'Paul says the magazine's sales are through the roof because of my angle,' Kasper said. 'So is online engagement, and I'm still on my basic office salary. Besides, I don't see why we can't all make hay while the sun shines.'

'I'm taking fifty per cent of whatever yen Pocari's giving you.'

'Twenty-five.'

'One hundred.'

'Okay, fifty. Listen, I went to the location you gave me, the one you traced from the missed call to the office. Nothing but a phone box in the middle of nowhere. Not a whiff of Dylan, which, frankly, was a relief because this thing's only just getting warmed up. And I've been thinking—'

'I don't pay you to think.'

'Hear me out. What if I find Dylan later today and he's alive and well? That would kill the story completely, wouldn't it?'

'I know, I know. This thing can't peak yet. I want to get at least one solid month out of it. The missing narrative is our exclusive, so we control the tap on the info. And it goes without saying, I need the coverage to run as long as possible. I need to approve each of your posts before they go live, okay? And when you find Dylan, we'll have him lie low for a while, then I'll peddle out the exclusive interview and homecoming extravaganza. We'll dedicate a whole issue to his return.'

'Then what?'

She sighed. 'I don't know.'

'Bear with me,' Kasper said. 'I've had this idea. Social media's mad for this story and it's starting to get coverage in major news outlets across the world. What would it be like if Dylan turned up, er, not alive?'

'If you mean dead, just say it.'

'Okay, dead. Suddenly, we'd have a ton of content. We'd run his obituary, of course, and I could make up various stories from his life.

I'd also interview his family and his friends – if he has any apart from Shultz, and I'm not sure about that connection. We could reprint his award-winning articles, retell the Iraq episode and piece together a memorial edition every year. We could even produce a documentary series for TV and publish a collection of his notes as a book. And that's just the start. It'd be like a tragic rock star gone-too-soon drama, and we'd own all the rights. We can spin that out for decades! And then there's the insurance money … Hello? Are you still there?'

'I am. Do you realise what you're saying?'

'It was just a thought. Sorry. Forget it, I—'

'Kasper.'

'I'm sorry. I know it's a bad idea.'

'And it's exactly the kind of idea that's going to make you the next chief editor.'

'What?'

'There's a good reason why I'm the youngest editor this publication has ever had. Who do you think orchestrated the kidnap in 2006 that saved this shitty magazine? Tell me about Shultz. He might be more useful than we thought.'

'I don't know what to say really. He doesn't say much, and maybe it's just reporter paranoia, but he strikes me as a man with less than positive intentions. He doesn't seem to know Dylan at all, and that's coming from me, and I only know Dylan from his articles.'

'Hmm, Dylan's articles have made him a lot of enemies over the years. He still gets death threats.'

'Really?'

'Really.'

That's what you got for covering controversial subjects and targeting the kind of people you didn't want as enemies. The hate mail was usually just incoherent bollocks sent from lunatics, but just one look at Dylan's back catalogue more than hinted at a list of reasons why people might be pissed off with him. Including Shultz.

'You know, Kasper, with these kinds of deals, you have to use what the universe gives you. So figure Shultz out and figure him in. He might be a good man to have around.'

THIRTY-THREE

It was exhausting – the guilt, the shame. He'd hit the gas hard, tried to outrun it, but the signs of a shattered civilisation were everywhere. He'd tried self-soothing with a mantra: There's nothing I can do to help. There's nothing I can do to help.

But was it true? He was a goddamn reporter. He should be covering this thing for the story.

Dylan pressed on anyway, and the landscape became less scarred the further north he drove. Nature began to resurrect itself – birds swooped through dancing trees and bathed in calm waters. He talked Mika into taking a break from teaching him Japanese so they could enjoy the crisp view.

'It's wonderful here,' she said. 'This could be my new happy place.'

The tarmac snaked around the edge of Lake Towada through land so manicured it looked as if it had been tended by giant hands. A fence of trees through which sunlight strobed gave way to sparkling blue water watched over by Mount Hakkōda. They cruised through a mountain tunnel and back out into brilliance, under bridges and around immaculate asphalt hairpins.

Mika had been right. The Towada-Hachimantai national park was nothing short of balm for the soul, though he couldn't help but find the contrast with the smoke, dust and anguish they'd seen along their way perverse. Still, life persisted, even in the face of disaster. It had to.

'It reminds me of Coniston in England,' he said, remembering youthful days kayaking and drinking in the late-summer sun. 'How's your ankle?'

'You know, ankle-y ... but it feels better.'

At the foot of the lake, there was a farmers' market next to a gift shop, a tourist centre and public amenities.

'Back in a second,' Mika said, and headed for the toilets.

Dylan people-watched – couples in matching weatherproof coats and sensible walking boots; families having uneasy conversations by their cars; a school bus full of children in fluorescent hats; a group of teenagers in flip-flops and sunglasses taking selfies.

'Solly! Dylan Solly!'

Across the car park, a teenager with yellow wraparound sunglasses on top of his head walked over. He said a few words in Japanese, threw an arm around Dylan and snapped a picture with his phone.

'Alright, chief,' Dylan said. 'I didn't expect to meet fans of niche journalism here, but for the record, I've no idea what the hell you're talking about. Next time, wait for permission before taking a picture, right?'

Mika returned as the young man gave Dylan the thumbs-up and walked away.

'Shall we go?' she said.

They left the crowds and went in search of wild land.

And found it. And isolation.

They strolled along the edge of a rippling stream and entered a deep forest where the air was floral and sweet.

'It's beautiful here,' Mika said, kneeling near a cluster of flowers. 'This is a horse-face flower.' She pointed to a pink perennial on top of a mound of tiny moss-green leaves. 'It's called that because when it blooms it looks like a horse's head.'

The colours were startling. Low blooms of violet, tangerine and rose; a plethora of green flora glinting with beads of moisture; brown trunks looming high overhead; above, an ocean of blue streaked with white.

'I feel like we've stumbled into an oil painting,' Dylan said as he plucked an orange flower and put it in Mika's hair. 'She walks in beauty, like the night ...'

'Mr Byron, I don't think anyone else knows about this place. It's like we're a million miles away from everything, like we're in a totally different life.'

'Mika, I know I can be a bore, and I'm sorry for that, but I'm glad you're here and I'm glad you brought us to this place.'

She took his hand and led him to a clearing in the valley of a volcano, home to a single thick-trunked tree with a heavy canopy and a steaming natural spring at its base.

Mika blushed, made him promise not to look, then stripped off and eased into the pool.

Dylan shook of his own his clothes and plunged in, letting the still, hot water swallow him whole. Mika looked radiant. She smiled, her body glistening in the light, and Dylan wondered if Adam and Eve could have ever been more content.

'It's like there's only you and me in the entire world,' he said. 'Despite all we've seen and all we've been through, I feel happy. Does that make me selfish?'

'Mr Byron?' Mika said. Her eyes were closed. Steam leapt off her shoulders where they met the waterline.

'Yeah?'

She opened an eye. 'You should kiss me.'

Some said a love that burns too bright blinds; others said intense love is akin to intense suffering. *Who cares?* he thought, and leaned towards her.

THIRTY-FOUR

Shultz pulled the blacked-out Ford Ranger into a service station car park just south of Sendai.

'So, where is he?' he said, a cigarette hanging off his lip. 'The payphone's given us nothing and the trail's gone cold. There's no point heading any further north; there isn't a goddamn soul on these highways.'

Kasper shrugged. 'That telephone booth back there was my only lead. Maybe it wasn't even Dylan who called the office. He might be dead after all.'

Shultz flicked his cigarette out of the window. 'He's alive, I guarantee it.'

'How can you be so sure?'

'I just know.'

'That's interesting. Apart from the few times I've seen him around the office, I only know Dylan by reputation, but you understand him as a friend, right? Where do you think he'd go? What kind of moves would he make? Does he associate with anyone else in Japan?'

Shultz chewed over the question and lit another cigarette. 'How the hell should I know?'

Kasper let a beat pass. 'Tell me again how you met him.'

Shultz put on a pair of brown, wire-framed sunglasses. 'You ask too many questions.'

'Habit of the job, I'm afraid,' Kasper said. 'Tell you what, a few words from an old friend of Dylan's would be great content for my blog. I'd be happy to hear the tale.'

Shultz hunkered low in his seat and glanced, left then right. 'I know him from here and there.'

Kasper took a white iPhone 4S from his pocket and scrolled through his Twitter feed. Anything to avoid looking directly at Shultz. 'That's a lie … isn't it?'

Shultz stiffened, then rummaged around in the glovebox.

'You know what I think?' Kasper said. 'I had this thought—'

Shultz laid a dull-grey snub-nosed Uzi on his lap, and Kasper recoiled.

'You don't have any more thoughts when you're around me, understand?' Shultz said. His face was creased, tight, serious. 'Here's the situation. I'll explain it so we're real clear. You're going to help me find Dylan Solly. Do that and stay out of my way, there's a chance you'll live.'

'Okay, okay. You want Dylan. I want a story. And I don't care how that story ends. Know what I mean?'

'Despite that stupid accent of yours, I think I understand you fine.'

'Either Dylan's alive or he's not. If we happen to find him dead, I'll buy his mother flowers. We're on the same side here, you and me. We both get what we need. And I'll keep my questions to myself, I promise. We can work together, I'm certain.'

'Okay. Let's assume your buddy Dylan is carryin' on north. My guess is he's sticking to the main roads. Why go north?'

'I've no idea,' Kasper said.

Shultz aimed the gun at Kasper's nose. 'What the hell are you good for? I don't need a tourist getting in my way. Get out of my car. Blood is hell on this interior.'

'Wait wait wait!' Kasper squealed. 'This could be a lead.' He held up the phone. A picture of a goofy kid with yellow sunglasses standing next to a dishevelled looking Dylan Solly. 'Looks like hashtag

SaveSolly just saved the day. It's tagged at Towada-Hachimantai national park.'

'That's a fair stretch. Okay, buckle up, asshole. You might be useful to keep around after all.'

Shultz hit the accelerator. The wheels spun on the gravel and the Ranger pulled out onto the northbound highway.

THIRTY-FIVE

Mika and Dylan left their clothes by the water's edge and set off into the ancient forest, steam rising from their naked bodies in the cool woodland. Wildlife scurried on the ground, the birds high above sang counterpoint, and a breeze swept underneath the tree canopy, cooling Mika's wet skin.

'Why would anyone ever leave such a splendid and unaffected place? I'd happily live here forever,' she said.

'That's crazy. What would you do for food?'

'I'd follow the animals and forage like they do, and I'd drink from the lake. I'd have everything I need. I would be wild!' She ran a few steps and pirouetted on her toes. 'And I'd be a friend to all the creatures.'

As the evening drew in, an early moon rose and the temperature fell. They headed back to the spring, dusted down their clothes and retraced their steps to the parking lot, now packed with day trippers preparing for the long drive home.

'I'm going to look in the gift shop before it closes,' Mika said, and sneered at Dylan's stained shirt. 'I hope they have T-shirts. We really need fresh clothes. I'll use the money Nao gave us. I won't be long.'

'Righto. I'm going to the bathroom. Meet you back here in a few.'

It was warm inside the store. Glass shelves displayed waving golden Maneki-neko cats of various sizes, colourful travel mugs, playful key rings, oversized Hello Kitty figurines, wooden back-scratchers, plastic bento boxes, lots of candy, and a series of travel books. For the artful shopper, a wall was hung with skilful landscapes of the park's mountains, hills, valleys and lakes. But no T-shirts.

She walked down the aisle, searching for an alternative souvenir, and glanced out the window. The lot was bathed in the glow of intersecting headlights, and a teenager in yellow sunglasses was talking to two gaijin – one spindly, spectacled and pointing to his phone, the other tall, muscular and furious, like some sort of American pro wrestler, the kind she'd seen on late-night TV. The boy pointed towards Dylan, who'd just emerged from the restroom.

The large man sprinted across the car park and tackled Dylan to the ground. His head bounced on the tarmac with a thud, and Mika whimpered. Then the man tied Dylan's wrists, covered his head with a sheet and threw him into the back of a blacked-out pickup.

THIRTY-SIX

Kasper sent a text to Sam. *Is the obituary piece ready?*

'As easy as that,' Shultz said, nodding towards the back seat where Dylan lay moaning and wriggling. 'Don't worry, son. We'll have you delivered in no time, then it's contract complete. Amen. But, hey, if it makes you feel any better, you're worth a lot of money to me – 50K US, so thanks, boy.'

'When he's dead, he'll be worth a lot more to me than 50,000 dollars, I can assure you,' Kasper said.

'Shut up, you waterhead bastard. We've still got work to do. We gotta get out of here. Not that there are any cops around. Shit. I better text the boss ... Where's my goddamn phone? Keep a look out.'

Kasper looked out each of the windows as the engine ticked over. 'Look, since we're both in deep now, you might as well tell me who you're working for.'

Shultz thumbed at his Nokia, and his face glowed green. Dylan groaned in the backseat. 'That's right, Dylan. You got your lil' buddy Kasper the-not-so-friendly ghost to thank for trackin' you down.'

'Don't tell him that, for fuck's sake. He could implicate me! I thought hitmen were meant to be discreet.'

'Don't worry, dickhead. I knocked him goofy.' Shultz gestured to the back seat. 'Look, he ain't even moving. Besides he'll be dead in a few hours, or maybe days, dependin' on what Jushin wants to do.'

Jushin? He'd heard that name before. Christ, of course. Jushin Okada.

'You're taking him to the Three?'

Shultz put down his phone. 'You gonna start blubbering now, princess, 'bout how you're gonna see your buddy Dylan being tortured in your dreams and you'll never forgive yourself.' Pussy.' He put the pickup in gear and slid out of the parking lot.

'Look,' Kasper said, 'give it to me straight. Do you think the Three would grant me an interview, as a thank-you for helping me find Dylan? You could ask on my behalf, in light of what a good team we make. It would be an international first.'

'I doubt it. Mostly 'cos it ain't three anymore.'

'What do you mean?'

'Last I heard, Shinsuke Takahashi's MIA. Now shut the fuck up, we gotta get south. I'll tell you what though, you are a mercenary, a pure cold-blooded, self-motivated mother. I'm beginning to like you, I am. So, I'll do you a solid and talk to the Three, er, Two, about that interview. But I warn you, if they wanna kill you, I'm not gonna stop 'em—'

A strobe of light cut through the cabin, metal crunched, and the window in the driver's-side door imploded, showering them with glass.

'What the fuck—' Shultz screamed.

Kasper's head slammed into the side of the pickup and airbag powder filled his nose and mouth. He coughed and spat, then shouted over the blare of the Ranger's horn. 'Shultz!'

The big guy didn't flinch, just sat, hunched forward, face buried deep in the deflating airbag.

The rear door opened, then slammed shut.

Kasper turned, looked in the back seat.

It was empty.

THIRTY-SEVEN

Mika's crumpled Suzuki lurched out of the car park. She could hear the bumper dragging along the ground. It caught under a wheel, and she glanced up into the rear-view mirror. It had detached and now lay on the smooth tarmac behind her. The dash was a constellation of amber and red. Both headlights were out and the road north was pitch dark.

Mika fought with the steering wheel as the Jimny hobbled over the clean tarmac, swerved around the lake and through the inky-black tunnel. A loud thump echoed on all sides. As soon as she hit a straight patch of highway, she floored the accelerator, then reached back and pulled the sheet off Dylan's head.

He looked ashen and frail. 'Holy shit, what the hell—' He pulled the thick plastic locking ties around his wrists. 'I can't get these fuckers off.'

'We have to get as far away as possible,' Mika said.

'I thought I was done for back there. Did you ram that huge truck with this little jeep?'

Too exhausted to reply, she concentrated on the road's centre line and keeping the car straight.

'Thank you,' Dylan said.

'We're not safe yet. We have to get away, keep going.' Blood poured from her nose.

'Mika, are you okay?'

'The airbags didn't go off.'

She couldn't focus. The world narrowed. She felt her hands slip from the slick steering wheel and everything went dark.

THIRTY-EIGHT

'Mika!'

The car veered dangerously close to the central reservation, and Dylan wrestled with the zip ties.

'Mika!'

The Jimny smashed into the concrete barrier and the world began to revolve. Sky, road, sky, road.

The car landed upside down. The windscreen shattered and there was an ear-splitting wail of steel grinding on tarmac.

Then silence.

They'd come to a stop on a grass verge. Acrid smoke billowed around the car, and Dylan groaned as pain shot through his back, shoulders, ribs. Even his ears stung.

'Mika,' he whispered.

Her eyes were closed and there was blood everywhere, though who it belonged to was anyone's guess – they were both covered in glass. At least the airbag had deployed this time, which had saved Mika from eating the steering column. She hung upside down, restrained by her safety belt, face cut and smeared with crimson.

He wriggled through the passenger window, dizzy and feeling the bite of glass on his chest. He willed himself to stay conscious and lumbered around the car to Mika.

He tried the door but it was wedged shut. Her lids flickered open.

'Undo your seatbelt,' he said, and tried to inhale. The pain made breathing difficult but a lack of oxygen was only adding to his light-headedness.

He kicked against the remaining glass in the window as Mika clunked down from her seat and pulled herself out. Dylan leant against the Suzuki's beaten panel work and focused on breathing.

'You okay?' he asked.

'I feel sick. You?'

He shook his head.

'There's a first-aid kit in the trunk.' She went to the boot, steadying herself against the car, blood dripping from her nose.

Dylan heard the smash of glass, then Mika returned with a small green pouch.

'I nearly killed us,' she said, and gnawed at the zip ties with scissors from the kit.

'Fuck!' He rubbed his wrists. 'You saved me back there.'

She rubbed her eyes and rummaged through the medical kit, then bandaged his head.

'You're cut too.' He pointed to her face and patched her up as best he could with cleansing wipes, cotton balls and Band-Aids.

The road was littered with glass and metal, and scarred where the Jimny had scraped a path to the verge.

'She needs more than a flipping-back on her wheels this time,' he whispered. Every breath felt caustic. He couldn't pull in enough air. 'I think we're fucked.'

THIRTY-NINE

Blood ran from Kasper's nose. He reached across and slapped Shultz. 'Come on, get up, you big American idiot.'

He slapped him again, and the big man lifted his head off the airbag. The horn stopped blaring.

Park visitors had gathered in front of the pickup, gawping and pointing at the truck.

'What the hell just happened?' Shultz drawled.

Kasper shrugged, and Shultz muttered something.

'I can't hear you,' Kasper said.

'I said no one damn well told me he had back-up. Did you know he had a partner?'

'How the hell could I?'

'If I find out you withheld intel from me, I'm gonna ...' Shultz tried to push the door open but it wouldn't budge. He kicked it free and yelled, 'What the hell are you all looking at?' at the gawkers.

'Come on,' Kasper said. 'We should get out there, catch up with them.'

Shultz went to the front of the Ford. 'Are you kidding me? They screwed up my truck. Look – they completely fucked it.'

'It's a bloody Ranger,' Kasper said. 'It's massive. It'll still go. Come on. They can't have gotten far. Dylan's escaped, and thanks to your big mouth he knows I'm involved. We need to finish the job. I thought you were good at this kind of thing.'

Shultz glared at him. 'I'm a professional! And no damn way am I going after them until I understand what just happened. I gotta get used to the idea that he's operating with someone who has balls of steel. That sombitch has to be crazy to pull off a stunt like that. Fucker could be some ol' Green Beret for all I know. We'd be walking into a trap.' Shultz walked a lap around his pickup. 'It's my fault. I should know better. A professional should always know his target. I gotta have every detail, otherwise shit like this happens.' He looked at the damage to the truck and rubbed his dirty-blond curly hair. 'Goddammit, look at that thang!' He swung open the door and stared at the back seat. 'I had him. He was right there. What the hell? Once they're in Black Beauty, they never escape. Man, now I got two sombitches to track down now – one for the boys and one for my Ranger.'

Kasper pinched his bloody nose. 'So what now?'

'Shut up your whining. That's what's now.'

'We're just going to sit here?'

'We're gonna regroup. I need to draw up a plan, you English prick. Hey, you friendly-useless-ass-ghost, you ever fired a gun?'

'I've used a paintball gun, and I did Laser Quest at my nephew's birthday. Is it like Laser Quest?'

'Gimme a break. Firing a *real* gun is no game, but even a moron like you can handle it. From now on, I need you to have my back. You ain't a passenger no more, got it? You're far from ideal ground support, but I got no one else at hand, so look sharp and get out.'

Kasper fell out of the car and staggered towards Shultz, who was rummaging in the boot.

'I've got a spare pistol or two in here.' He lifted the liner. Beneath was an arsenal of automatic rifles, shotguns and pistols, complete with ammunition. 'Now, all we need is someplace remote. That shouldn't be too difficult around here.'

'For what?' Kasper said, backing away.

'For your fucking firearms training, dumbass.' Shultz picked out two pistols and a box of rounds, and slammed the door. 'Kasper, we gotta get ready for a good ol' fashioned manhunt.'

FORTY

Nao's blankets were the only shield from the cold as Mika cradled Dylan through the night. Minute by minute, her strength dissolved until the dew of morning touched her face.

An engine approached and stopped close by. A door slammed. There were footsteps nearby. Her body had seized up. Everything hurt. And she was exhausted.

No way could they run. She blinked. It was all she could manage.

'Hello. My name's Dylan Solly. Can you help?'

An elderly man stood over them, clean-shaven, slight, worried creases around his eyes.

'Dylan,' she whispered, 'You just spoke Japanese.'

'I know, but you'll have to take it from here. I'm all out of words.'

The stranger pointed to the car wreck. 'You're either very lucky or very unlucky. Whichever it is, let me help. I'm Zenji. Can you get up?'

'Just about. Can you take us to a hospital?' Mika said.

'I can drive you to Aomori City Hospital.'

They sat in a tractor among clattering farm tools that jostled with each bump and turn. After a few miles on winding roads, they entered a town full of fuji apples – painted on fences, windows, park benches and bus stops. A truck full of red shiny fruit drove by and Mika inhaled the fresh fragrance. White clouds hovered in a honey-crisp sky, and sunlight shafted through branches of ambrosia.

'Ah, the sun always shines on the righteous. You okay?' Dylan said.

She sighed. It was the third time he'd asked that question. 'Better than you, I think.'

'Are we going to a hospital?'

'We are. Now rest.'

'How far are we from your mother's place? A few miles?'

'No. Like I said before, we're still far away, maybe seven or eight hundred kilometres.'

'Why would my magazine be trying to kill me? I heard them in the car back there … the Three's hitman and Kasper.'

'I don't know. Now calm yourself. Save your strength.'

'Where are we going? Are you okay? Are we near your mum's?'

'We're nearly at the hospital.'

It couldn't come soon enough.

FORTY-ONE

'That's the first time I've ever been turned away from a hospital,' Dylan said. His head was still pounding and his breath laboured.

'You don't have medical insurance and you're considered non-critical. Unless you want a huge bill,' Mika said.

'Oh, what a day ... and what a night.' He slumped against the corridor wall and slid to the floor as a nurse rushed a woman in a wheelchair to a room. It appeared the wards were still dealing with people who'd been injured in the quake. 'I guess they don't have time for a gaijin with no insurance. I'm glad they fixed you up though. You feeling better?'

Mika's bandage-swaddled hands looked huge, and her face was a patchwork of small circular Band-Aids.

'I am. I got you more bandages and bought these with the last of our money. It cost almost everything we had.'

She handed over three boxes – codeine, ibuprofen, and paracetamol.

'Thanks. I'd be so screwed without you.' He tore open the boxes and dry swallowed a handful of pills.

'Well, I'd be stuck in Tomioka without you. So we're probably even.' She tried to laugh and slid down next to Dylan. 'Well, not quite. I had to put a home address on the form. I had no idea what to write. I'm homeless.'

They stood, and Dylan leaned heavily on Mika until they reached a bench in the hospital grounds. Mika filled their water bottles from a drinking fountain, and Dylan wrapped himself in a blanket and inspected their supplies, which Mika had wrapped up in the other blanket.

'Our inventory's looking poor,' he said.

'What's left?'

'The remains of a first-aid kit, some pills and the new dressing, a few of Nao's bento boxes … that's it. How are we for cash?'

Mika pulled a few notes and coins from her pocket and grimaced. 'Hardly anything.' She gulped from one of the water bottles. 'I called my car insurance. They'll pick up my Suzuki and process the claim, but they can't offer a courtesy car.'

'Oh dear.'

'But remember your promise. You said you'd get me to my mom's house, so we need a plan.'

'Let's hire a car,' Dylan said, snuggling deeper into the blanket.

'We don't have enough money, and we'd need ID. Do you have any?'

'Yeah, in my wallet.' He patted his pockets. 'Shit. I lost it. I got nothing.'

'Same.'

He felt woozy again. 'How far away did you say your mother's place is?'

'Eight hundred kilometres or so.'

'How about a train?'

'Trains are expensive. We can't afford even one ticket.'

'Let's just jump on and steal a ride. We'll play dumb if we get caught.'

'I don't even know if the trains are running after the earthquake. And riding them illegally is a one-way ticket to jail.'

'Strict over here, isn't it?' He breathed in, and out, trying to ignore the pain. 'How about we visit your bank?'

'No bank card.'

'I called the British embassy when you were getting treatment,' Dylan said. 'They can sort me out with an emergency passport for £100, and it will take up to three weeks to process, so I should pay, then check back. Apparently, they have no legal obligation to help me beyond that. I tried phoning my old flatmate from years ago, Bobby. No answer – I guess it's around 11 p.m. in London so he'll be staggering home from the pub. But he might be able to wire me money or book tickets in my name if I can get hold of him. Thing is, I won't be able to collect anything without a passport or driver's licence. Where are we again?'

'Aomori. It's a port town, northern Honshu on the Japanese mainland. We need to cross the Tsugaru Strait to get to Hokkaido, then cross the whole country to get to my mom's in Cape Sōya.'

'A strait? Water? That means a ferry.'

'Which we can probably afford – it's pretty cheap – but then what?'

'We'll hitch a ride. How's Japan for hitchhiking?'

'I've no idea.'

He took Mika's hand. 'Well, let's find out. It's Cape Sōya or bust, or maybe jail. But first, let's relax here and let the painkillers kick in.'

FORTY-TWO

Kasper and Shultz cruised north along Route 102. The Ford's engine squealed, and the right-hand headlight dangled over the bumper, or what was left of it; half of it was stowed in the rear hold.

Shultz chomped on a breakfast sandwich, one hand on the steering wheel. 'So, let's make sure we're clear on the new plan. What's the first thing you do when we get a visual on the target?'

'Engage the enemy,' Kasper said, typing updates into his latest blog post. 'And more importantly, I get an exclusive interview with Jushin and Freddie.'

'We take him alive if we can – I'll get more money that way. But if things go south, remember what I said – do *not* hesitate. And this is important – *squeeze* the trigger like I showed you. Don't pull on it like it's your daddy's teeter, got it?'

Kasper nodded and touched the tender flesh around his bruised eyes. A bloody tissue plugged his nose.

'That's my boy,' Shultz said. 'Pistol Kasper! Or Kasper the Hitman, Kasper the … We'll figure out a new nickname down the line.'

'What about Killer Kasper?'

'Not bad!'

'What's your nickname?'

'They used to call me Doctor Death. Don't know why – I used to be a plumber.'

'Maybe because Doctor Death sounds better than The Toilet Unclogger or The Pipe Unburster.' Kasper closed his laptop and leaned his head against the window. 'What the hell is that?'

A trail of metal and plastic trailed over the road ahead.

'Well, shit, that looks like a fucked-up getaway car to me – a fucked-up little upside-down jeep that was heading north, for that matter. Get a hold of your gun. I have reason to believe this is our time to strike.'

'Now?'

'That goddamn tiny white car has Ford-black paint scratched across its bumper.'

Shultz hit the brakes, jumped out and vaulted over the ruined central reservation. He lifted the Uzi and strafed the Suzuki, then aimed through the driver's window and skulked around the grass verge.

'Shit!' He spat at the ground.

'I told you we should have chased them last night.'

'And walk into a potential ambush? You're a rookie. And a complete asshole. You hear me, asshole? No, this is good. This'll do fine.'

'How can this possibly *do fine?*'

'Because where would you go after a wreck like this?'

'I don't know, Disneyworld?'

'Think, asshole. That's your new nickname by the way.'

'I suppose you'd go to a hospital. Which is where I'd like to be right now.'

'Boom. Correctamundo. Now shut up, saddle up and find me directions to the nearest medical facility on that fancy phone of yours.'

FORTY-THREE

The three-kilometre walk to the ferry terminal was rough going, and night was setting in as Dylan and Mika limped to the ticket office. Mika checked the prices on the board outside the booth and recounted their remaining yen twice. They could afford two tickets, one-way, though it would cost them all they had, a fact she didn't trouble Dylan with given his declining health.

Water sloshed beneath the gangplank. Black-tailed gulls squawked overhead, and a cold wind blew. The blare of the foghorn signalled they were finally on their way to Japan's northernmost island.

The ferry was clean, modern and seemingly deserted. Only the purr of the ship's engines suggested there was other life on board. Long mirrors reflected carpeted floors and large empty spaces.

'It's like a ghost ship,' Mika whispered.

They trudged down a narrow stairwell to the lower deck and a series of large, doorless rooms. At the entrance to one was a pair of shoes so Mika led them to the next space. Dylan slumped against the wall and slid down onto the smooth blue carpet.

'I need to sit up. It's too painful to lie down,' he said. 'But the peace and quiet's nice. I feel like we're actually getting somewhere, and we can finally rest.'

'Your breathing seems easier now.'

He put an arm around her. 'I've just got to catch my breath.'

She lay down, felt the gentle throb of the diesel engines and the gently undulating ocean. Mercifully, sleep came.

FORTY-FOUR

S hultz leaned over the reception desk and spoke in Japanese. 'Look, sir, you are talkin' to an officer of the American Central Intelligence Agency. That's C-I-A. The *American* CIA. And he's Interpol.' He pointed at Kasper. 'You want that kind of heat? Do you enjoy being the guy standing in the way of the international pursuit of a wanted criminal?'

'I'm sorry, sir. I can't give you confidential patient data.'

'I'm not asking for data.' Shultz pulled down his sunglasses and glared over the top of the rim. 'I'm asking for *information*. Specifically relating to an escaped prisoner who's wanted on extradition charges for multiple orphan homicides. Are you in favour of killing children, sir? Do you realise this is a diplomatic incident involving dead Japanese babies?'

Kasper rested his palms on the desk, leant into Shultz and said, 'I don't speak Japanese, but I can tell this isn't going well. Allow me to cut through the bullshit.' He pushed a pile of banknotes across the marble countertop. 'Now politely tell him I'd like to know if an Englishman named Dylan Solly has been here within the past twelve hours – it's that simple.'

Shultz glared at the clerk. 'You know what I wanna know.'

The clerk scanned the corridor, placed a hand over the money and slipped it into his pocket. With a deep breath he began typing.

'Here we go – Mr Solly, Dylan. No local address, English tourist. Head injuries resulting from a car crash. Non-critical. He was not insured and did not receive treatment, but his partner did.'

'Who's the partner?' Shultz said.

The clerk raised an eyebrow. Shultz sighed and pulled a screwed-up bill from his tracksuit, and threw it at the computer.

The clerk pocketed the crumpled note. 'Treated for concussion. Wrist and hand injuries, minor cuts and scrapes resulting from a car accident. Twenty-six years old. Name … let me see … Mika Ito. Address listed as Cape Sōya. She had no ID but her insurance—'

Shultz punched the desk. 'Say that again!'

'Her insurance was able to verify. It's normal practice when—'

'No, goddammit, the name.'

The clerk rambled about having to refresh the page, how the computer was slow, some or other server issue he'd called IT support about three times. Shultz was about to punch the whining asshole when the man spoke.

'I have it here. Yes. Mika Ito.'

Shultz rubbed his chin. 'Well I'll be a sombitch …'

'What is it?' Kasper said.

'I don't believe my goddamn luck.'

'What'd he say?'

'Your buddy is ridin' with a woman.'

'You know her?'

'Is a frog's ass watertight?'

Kasper looked confused.

'To use your Queen's English, yessir, you're goddamn right I know her. At least I know enough about her to understand that we have a problem.'

FORTY-FIVE

Shultz blew cigarette smoke out of the window of the idling Ranger. They were still in the car park and Kasper was trying to work out why.

'Shut up, Kasper! I can hear you thinking over there. Goddammit, what did I tell you about that? Papa's gotta concentrate. The boys are chasing my ass to get the target to them asap. Some sort of rush job, and now this—'

'Greensleeves' erupted from his pocket. Kasper glanced at the Nokia's screen. It read *Jushin*.

'Fuck, here we go again.'

Shultz put the phone to his ear. 'No! You listen to me. The job isn't done yet. It's got real complicated. The target's lost and we need to talk. Wait – what do you mean? Well, holy shit is all I can say ... So why do you need this guy so quick? Practice? ... What does that mean? Damn! Why didn't you tell me this before?' Shultz ran his eyes over Kasper and took another drag. 'Okay. In that case, if that's the bind you're in, I have an idea. Kinda. Let's just say it'll satisfy your most pressing requirement. And tell Freddie to calm the fuck down. I can hear him yelling back there.'

'What the hell was that all about?' Kasper said.

'New information. Sharpen your pencil. It looks like you're getting that interview sooner than you thought.'

FORTY-SIX

'**D**id you sleep okay?' Dylan rubbed his eyes.

Mika yawned. 'I think so. I wonder what the time is. We must be near Hokkaido by now.'

They headed for the bathrooms and Dylan rinsed some of the blood from his clothes and aired them under the hand dryer.

'It's time to replace your head dressing,' Mika said. 'It's full of blood.' She pulled a clean white roll of bandage from the first-aid kit. 'This is the last one, so don't bleed too much.'

'At least we got good use out of that kit,' Dylan said, and scanned their supplies. 'Let's hope we don't have any more accidents. We'll need to pick some up some food too. We've got a long journey ahead.'

'And no car. Sit still, will you?'

'Hey, Mika.'

He stole a kiss. She shooed him off and they headed for the upper deck and the night sky. The nearest stars were like bright balls of blue-white fire on a bed of intergalactic dust. The sea air blew Mika's hair about her eyes as she looked up.

'Something about the ocean air and the stars makes me feel good,' she said. 'Look over there. That's Hakodate.'

The ferry sailed into the port and they disembarked. Dylan spotted a payphone.

'Get the operator to direct a call to my office. I'll give you the number.'

'I taught you numbers. I'll speak to the operator. You give them the numbers.'

Despite his stumbling Japanese, he was connected, and this time his call was answered.

'Good morning. You've reached the reception of *Topic International Magazine*. Violet speaking. How may I direct your enquiry?'

'Violet, it's Dylan.'

'Oh my God! I'll patch you right through to Sam. I've been worried sick.'

'Wait. Don't transfer me, and keep quiet! You're the only person I want to talk to right now. And do me a favour – don't mention this call to anyone.'

'What? Why?'

'Because I don't want anyone to know where I am. It sounds crazy, and I'm fuzzy on the details thanks to a heavy concussion, but I'm pretty sure Kasper, with the help of a hitman, is trying to kill me. And I think Sam's involved.'

'No!'

'Yes. Like I said, I don't have the facts yet, but something's wrong. My reporter's nose is twitching.'

'Why would Sam do that?' Violet whispered.

'Probably to sell magazines, knowing her. I'll be honest, this whole situation has brought back some old doubts. There are some things about what happened in Iraq all those years ago that just never added up. I've had my suspicions over the years, just nothing I could verify or do anything about. I put it down to paranoia, but now, I don't know.'

'Like what?'

'Like Sam set up the assignment that led to the kidnapping in Iraq. I didn't think the story was even worthwhile chasing, but she insisted we cover it. I've always wondered why she was so damn adamant that Geoff and I had to do it on that particular day at that particular time. And what took her so long to get the ransom money together? I pushed all this stuff to the back of my mind until about twenty-four hours ago.'

'I wouldn't put it past her. What are you going to do?'

'It's what *you're* going to do that's important.'

'Me? I can't do anything.'

'You can do plenty. First, this conversation needs to stay strictly between us. Second, I want you to dig up any information you can find about an American hitman operating in Japan – goes by the name of Shultz. Sorry, I know it's not a lot to go on but—.'

'A man with that name phoned here a few days ago. He was asking after you. Sam said he was your friend.'

'He isn't. Do you know what they spoke about?'

'No, but there's a way I can find out. Sam records all her calls.'

'Do you have access?'

'I back them up once every six weeks or so. She keeps the recorder on her desk; it's wired up to her phone twenty-four seven.'

'Do me a favour, go get the data off that thing. All of it. And send it to my personal email, not my work one.'

'I can't just sneak into her office.'

'Who says you can't? Come on, Violet. I need that information.'

'But that would be stealing – I can't do that. I never even take the free sugar packets from Starbucks. Besides, Sam practically lives in her office. I don't think she even goes home some nights.'

'It's not stealing, it's borrowing. And we can easily get her out of her office.'

'How?'

'What does she love to do?'

'Bully the staff.'

'And after she's bored with that?'

'She goes shopping.'

'Exactly.'

FORTY-SEVEN

Dylan hung up. It was 10 p.m. He surveyed their surrounds – a tarmac road, a series of dark industrial buildings and the smell of fish.

'It's not exactly what I'd call a destination city.'

'I guess it's the kind of place you pass through,' Mika said.

'Then it should be perfect for hitchhiking. Let's take a peek down at the main road over there.'

They hobbled a few blocks and arrived at a retail park with a flood-lit 7-Eleven.

'The first rule of hitchhiking,' he said. 'Find a 7-Eleven and stick out a thumb. A petrol station or service station is a good second option. And always appear smart and approachable, but not weak.' He checked his reflection in the store's window. Bandaged head, dirty shirt, swollen eyes. 'I look like total shit, but you present much better.'

Mika turned to the window and pushed back strands of hair. 'I'm not sure about that. I have cuts all over my face. We look like trouble. I don't think anyone'll stop for us. You hitchiehiked before?'

Dylan giggled, corrected her, then told her about how he'd back-packed across Hong Kong in the mid-nineties with Geoff. 'That was a very long time ago, a whole different life.'

'When you were younger and stupider.' She laughed. 'I know so little about you.'

'We've got around seven hundred kilometres of road ahead of us. By the time we get where we're going, I'm sure we'll know everything about each other.'

'And what if you learn something you don't like? Something bad.'

A Honda approached them and Dylan stuck out his thumb and offered his best smile. The driver peered at him, grimaced and hit the accelerator.

'We might be here a while,' he said. 'Sorry, you were saying?'

Mika took a breath. 'Let's use the time to teach you more Japanese. It'll help you on the road. There aren't many gaijin up north.'

'Talk to me in Japanese. It'll tune my ear.'

She pointed at items in 7-Eleven's window and named them. 'Say what I say.'

For the next ninety minutes, Dylan repeated her words and Mika laughed at his pronunciation.

'Now, repeat after me. Kisu shite ku re baka.'

'What does it mean?'

'That means kiss me, you idiot.'

He leaned in.

Tyres screeched. A door opened. Someone yelled. Something gripped Dylan's shoulder and there was a *thwack* as pain lanced through the back of his head.

FORTY-EIGHT

Dylan fell forward and twisted around, searching for his attacker. A blow to his crotch took the wind out of him. He grunted, and fell on one knee.

What the fuck?

Standing over him was an elderly woman, no more than five foot tall. She wore a thick leopard print overcoat, leather trousers, her head a mass of artificial red curls.

He caught her follow-up punch and introduced himself in frustrated Japanese.

'You English?' the woman snapped in English.

'Hai.'

'You speak like English.'

Her expression was furious, but at least she'd stopped punching him. She spoke to Mika, her words short and sharp. Mika's reply seemed to calm the woman, and her fury morphed into a more general sense of irritation. Dylan, now more confused than hurt, rubbed his head and stood, trying to not make a big deal out of his busted balls.

'She thought you were a Russian rapist,' Mika said.

'Russians come to Hokkaido to steal and rape,' the woman shrieked. 'Be careful. What are you doing here? What happened to her face? And your head? You been fighting?'

Mika told her about their car wreck and their plan to hitchhike to Cape Sōya.

'You're crazy, but okay. Get in, English. I take you as far as Sapporo.' She marched towards her car.

'Does everybody hate Russians around here?' Dylan whispered as they walked towards the woman's car.

'No,' Mika said. 'Some people hold on to historic disputes. Manchuria, the overlapping border between Russia, China and Japan, has a long history of such things. Fighting there led to the 1904 Russo–Japanese War. Old-world problems.'

They got into the back seat and strapped themselves in.

'I've never seen a car like this,' Mika said.

'1970. Datsun 510,' the woman barked.

It was a boxy thing, mint green, lashings of chrome over the grill and windows, and mirrors mounted on the wings.

'Ninety-six horsepower!' she said, looking at Dylan with an air of defiance. She revved it, and left it in first gear until the engine screamed.

'My name is Baba. Call me Betty. Now, English, we practice my British accent. Ziss is a pen!' she said as she sped chaotically along the highway.

'*This* is a pen.' Dylan said, meeting her gaze through the slip of a rear-view mirror.

'I take every chance to improve my English,' Betty said, 'but I never meet English people. Where is your tie? All English wear tie. Are you sure you are not Russian?'

'I'm sure, and call me Dylan.'

'Diran. Why you go north?'

Mika explained.

'You're stupid,' Betty said. 'Cape Sōya is very far, very empty, very cold. Edge of the world. From Cape Sōya, you can see all the way to Russia and America and … Bulgaria. I know. I went there one time – big mistake. Very boring.'

Mika leant into him and whispered, 'Despite the questionable geography lesson, this hitchiehike is good. Sapporo's a good three hundred kilometres north.'

The journey frayed Dylan's nerves. The rain was coming down in sheets and Betty kept the temperature inside the car set at sweltering. The windows fogged, impairing Betty's vision. Worse, her roadcraft seemed almost non-existent. More than once, Dylan's foot pressed down on an invisible brake as Betty turned late into almost every corner. Only Mika's company distracted him from the death ride.

Betty stared at them through the rear-view mirror. 'You in love?'

Dylan looked at Mika, studying her expression.

'I was in love once,' Betty said. 'Big mistake. You know English well? How long you know him?'

'I think it's been two days,' Mika said.

'Oh, no. No. Not long enough. We stop now.'

She hit the brakes, and they came to a juddering halt on a patch of road high in the hills. Dylan and Mika were thrown forward, then back into the seat.

'Get out. Get out now.'

'You're joking, right?' Dylan said.

'Out! Out!'

He was too tired to argue, and opened the door and stepped onto a gloomy mountain road overlooking Hakodate.

FORTY-NINE

'At least it's a picturesque spot to be deserted in,' Dylan said. And it had stopped raining a few minutes earlier.

'It's a little remote,' Mika said. 'Let me talk with her. Maybe I can reason with her.'

'Please do. Our chances of getting a ride from here are exactly zero, especially at this hour. And any cars that do drive past won't notice us because it's so dark.'

Betty got out of the car, lit a cigarette and took him by the arm.

'Look here.' She pointed her smoking hand at a glowing orange dot to the south, where they'd come from. 'See those?'

'The streetlights on the highways?'

'Yes. What do you see?'

'Streetlights on a highway.'

She slapped his arm. 'Stupid English. What do you *see*?'

He looked. The distant highway glowed furnace yellow. A few cars with twinkling factory-red tail lights moved along it. A brighter spot morphed into an hourglass shape. He reported his observations.

'You can understand a person by what they see in the lights of Hakodate,' Betty said. 'You afraid of time – you worry how it passes. You scared life short. For you, maybe it will be.' She took another drag and the tip glowed red. 'Mika, what you see?'

'I see a wine glass.'

'Of course, you are drunk on love!' Betty puffed again and exhaled a cloud of smoke.

'English,' she said through the haze, 'you know some Japanese. The most important words you must learn are these – "Musume san to kekkon sasetekudasai."'

'What does that mean?'

'It means, "May I marry your daughter?" Very important in Japan to ask for permission from father. You must bow on your knees and ask him. Understand?'

'And if I don't?'

She closed her eyes, whispered what sounded like a prayer, walked over to Mika and kissed her on the forehead. 'Then you are not blessed.'

FIFTY

Betty drove them along roads flanked by bamboo grass. An abandoned farm nestled in the sea of green. A half-moon had sunk to the bottom of a lake, overlooked by the surrounding mountains. They left the farms behind and approached the suburbs of Sapporo, accompanied by silver rain.

'It's late,' Betty said. 'You can stay with me. I don't want the Russians to get you, Mika.'

Dylan's head and chest hurt, and breathing was still difficult. But mostly he was dog-tired and ready for bed.

Betty looked over her shoulder as she strode to the front door. She unlocked bolts, latches, bars and clasps, gestured for them to join her inside and flicked the lights. 'No sex in my house!'

'We appreciate the shelter,' Mika said, holding Dylan upright.

'I'm old-fashioned. Get married, you can do what you want. Not before. Drink this.' Betty gave Dylan a bottle of whisky.

'You both sleep down here. I wake you at seven. And English – you steal from me, I kill you.'

She climbed the stairs and slammed her bedroom door. There was a *thunk* – the door being locked, Dylan presumed.

'Are you an early riser?' Mika said.

'I'm up early most days.'

'I like my pillow too much. I sleep late when I can.'

'You sound like my cousin. He enjoys a lie-in more than anyone I've ever known,' Dylan said, settling on the couch. 'He would snooze the whole day away. I mean it, he could sleep through a hurricane. I don't know how he does it.'

'Tell me about him.' Mika snuggled next to him, her ear to his chest.

'He's younger than me. Lazier too, but he's talented. My father says his side of the family are riff-raff, but I like them. He's a DJ, and he's pretty good, though I don't think I've ever told him. He has this one song I love. "Churchill" it's called. Anyway, he's just signed a big record deal and I'm proud of him, even though I don't show it.' He unscrewed the bottle of booze. 'Whisky?'

She shook her head. 'I've never tried it.'

'I think I might be a little jealous of him,' Dylan said. 'He's really creative, not like me. I'm too vain to be creative in that way. I just write what I see and call it how it is. But Drew has an exciting life ahead of him. I wonder about his future, this megastar DJ. Where will he be ten years from now? Probably living large in California. He loves the idea of LA – it's the land of milk and honey, he says.'

'And where will *you* be ten years from now?'

Dylan laughed. 'I've no idea. Hopefully not sleeping on Betty's couch.' He took another slug. 'But in all seriousness, I see nothing. It's a blank. But I hope I'm happy. I hope it works out.'

'You hope what works out?'

'Don't make me spell it out.' His lips neared hers.

'NO SEX!' Betty yelled above them.

But it was too late.

FIFTY-ONE

Dylan's time in Sapporo began with a magpie tapping on Betty's living-room window.

Betty marched down the stairs, tying her dressing gown and cursing. She pulled a bag from a set of drawers in the hall, opened the front door and threw seed on the ground outside. It was bang on seven.

'Clever bird,' Mika said.

'You live here alone, Betty?' Dylan said.

'No. Me and the bird. You want breakfast too?' She threw a little seed over Dylan.

'I like you, Betty. You're bonkers.'

The cottage was cosy. The exposed hand-cut wooden beams, stone fireplace, rendered walls and tiled floor reminded Dylan of an old English Tudor farmhouse. Dylan half-expected Heathcliff to storm in and grind his teeth in a fit of love-fuelled ill temper. But there was only Betty, smiling through the open door, feeding a hungry magpie with a handful of seed.

'You still going to Cape Sōya?' Betty said.

Dylan nodded.

They ate, and Betty poured tea. A newspaper was slipped through the letterbox, and she retrieved it.

'So terrible. So much damage. So many dead.'

She pushed it towards Dylan.

'I've learned how to speak a little Japanese but I can't read a word of it.' He passed it to Mika.

She scanned the pages and shook her head. '"City left abandoned," this headline says. "Known for its beautiful blossoms, Tomioka was forced to evacuate, displacing thousands of residents." There's a discussion about military support being increased to search for survivors along the east coast. They have pictures. Look at Tomioka now. It's tragic.'

There were three photographs: the beached boat they'd passed on the way out of Tomioka; an aerial shot of the town, reduced to a mudslide; and a three-storey carcass of a concrete office block surrounded by rubble, timber and its roof. It was where Dylan had seen the old man with long grey hair and dark Himmler glasses. The beam Shinsuke Takahashi had been pinned under was visible, but the man himself had gone. Dylan searched every inch of the photograph. Where the hell was he? There'd been no reports about him being found. Surely that would have been news.

Dylan tuned back into the conversation.

'How will you get there? North?' Betty asked.

'We plan to continue hitchhiking,' Mika said. 'Can you drive us to the centre of Sapporo? We might find a ride there.'

Betty nodded. 'Sure, and hey, English, if you see Buddha on the road, kill him.'

'What?'

'It's an old saying,' Mika said. 'It means don't rely on a teacher for enlightenment.'

FIFTY-TWO

Shultz walked into the dingy apartment and declared, 'Jushin, Freddie, allow me to present plan B.'

'It's about damn time you got here!' Okada said.

'Who the hell's this?' Yoka said, looming over Kasper.

'Er, Shultz, can you translate for me?' Kasper said.

Shultz ignored him. 'You said you needed a living body, and he's got one.'

Kasper looked up at Yoka and gave a nervous wave. 'Hi. My, you are large. You must be Freddie, and you're Jushin. Nice to meet you both. I'm here to interview you. Do you speak English? Where should I set up? Who's that? Oh my God, is he dead?'

In the shadows, illuminated by the green, yellow and blue waveforms of a ventilator's monitor, lay Shinsuke Takahashi. An IV had been plugged into his forearm. His eyes were sunk under half-closed lids, just visible above a fogged-up oxygen mask.

'Fuck! He's alive?' Shultz said.

'Barely,' Okada said.

'You think he'll make it?'

'It doesn't look good. We found him in Tomioka, close to death, trapped under wreckage. He's lucky he didn't bleed out. He's even luckier he didn't get pneumonia. He's a tough old boy, we already knew that, but sepsis has set in. We've been keeping it at bay with

130

antibiotics, but we're losing the battle. We've only got one option left.'

'What is this, some kind of makeshift hospital?' Kasper said.

Shultz turned to Okada. 'Why do you need a body?'

'Practice ...' Takahashi croaked behind his mask.

'I've no choice but to perform the operation myself,' Okada said. 'His leg must be amputated, but I've never done anything like it before. Shinsuke has the knowledge, so he'll talk me through a practice run so I'll be ready for his operation. We must do it soon.'

Next to Takahashi's bed, a row of tools lay on a silver tray – three scalpels, a fine-toothed bone saw, dissection scissors, forceps, needle holders, a curved lifting-back metacarpal saw, a butcher saw, a Gigli cutting wire with two wide handles, a tourniquet, and a bottle of povidone iodine. A shelf behind was stacked with bandages, paper tape, gauze pads, stretchable kling roll, Adaptic dressing and black nitrile gloves.

'You're gonna chop off his leg here?' Shultz said.

'Can someone tell me what's going on?' Kasper said.

Yoka kicked his chair across the room. 'We don't have time for all this talk. Let's get it over with.' He wrapped his hands around Kasper's throat and squeezed.

Kasper's knees buckled.

Kasper came to. His left leg felt heavy and cold. He strained his neck and looked down. A tourniquet had been wrapped around it. He was naked and lying on some sort of metal work surface. Handcuffs bound his wrists and ankles. A single lightbulb hung above him.

Okada stood by a tool tray, wearing a leather smock and rubber gloves that reached his elbows. He exchanged words with Takahashi, who talked at length with a wavering, weak voice.

'What are you saying?' Kasper squealed. 'Speak English! What are you doing? You can't do this to me. I'm a journalist!'

Takahashi murmured. And under a cloud of cigarette smoke, in a seat by the wall, Shultz translated.

'The old man says he has to have his leg amputated. That it's a lifeless appendage, dead and gangrenous. He laments the things he must endure for the sake of life, and … and that in all Jushin's dealings – that's the man who's about to cut you – he's never had to amputate anything before. Can you believe that shit? So he needs practice, and you're it. And he said somethin' about your life being a worthy sacrifice.'

Okada draw a thick, black marker line around Kasper's thigh.

'Stop!'

'Jushin says to wish him luck,' Shultz said.

'No! Please! Shultz! Do something!' Kasper fought against the restraints as the Merchant pinched his soft skin, halfway up his femur.

'Oh, by the way,' Shultz said, 'they're saving the painkillers and anaesthesia for the ol' boy, so this is gonna hurt like hell. But if you don't die of shock, you'll survive – that's if he cuts your leg off properly and treats your wound. Keep calm and good luck, pal. I'm rooting for ya.'

Okada picked up a scalpel, and Kasper began to scream.

FIFTY-THREE

Shultz walked back in the room too soon. The screaming had stopped. Okada knelt at Takahashi's bedside, holding Kasper's disembodied leg.

'You are ready,' Takahashi said. 'As am I.'

'It is an honour to serve you,' Okada replied.

Takahashi looked grey and small. 'The time is now, though I fear I'm more prepared for life than death, and which one I face is uncertain. You've always been good to me, Jushin, a wonderful student, like a son … If I leave this world, my empire is yours.' He choked back a coughing fit. 'But if I live, there's one thing I'll need more than life itself. Don't judge me.' He lifted a photograph pressed to his chest and offered it to Okada with trembling hands. 'After we escaped from prison, I tried to find her, but failed. Bring her to me.' His eyes closed and his head fell back on the pillow.

Okada dropped the leg and handled the picture as if it were pure gold. It was of Yonomori Park in full bloom. Amid the blues, greens and pinks stood a mother and teenage daughter.

'That's what I came to talk about,' Shultz said.

'You know these people?' Okada said.

'That woman's his ex. The girl's his daughter. For the past seven years, Shinsuke Takahashi's hired me to be her guardian. Once every six months, I check in on her and report back to the ol' fella. His orders are always the same, and he's very strict on this – be invisible. Observe. Deal with any problems she has. And bring any fancy man of hers to meet him. Not that she's had any while I've been watching.'

'*Meet* him?'

'He'd kill him, of course. It's just a question of how fast or slow. You know how Shinsuke rolls.'

'Why?'

'Because after the divorce he went full-time psychopath. Couldn't maintain a typical father–daughter relationship, you know? Life sucks like that. Anyhow, the girl wanted nothing to do with him, which didn't help. She built a whole new life without him.'

'He loves her, but he kills her lovers?'

'He's a funny ol' guy, ain't he? The money's good so I don't ask questions. He once said something about not wanting her to die from a broken heart or some shit.'

'He never said a word to me.'

'Don't feel bad.' Shultz put an arm around Okada. 'Me and the old man go way back. He had a whole different life then. He even had this sister—'

'Had?'

'She passed on a while ago. That's all I know. But whatever happened, it made him very protective of his little girl.'

Okada put the photo into the pocket of his blood-stained shirt.

'And that reminds me,' Shultz said. 'Funny story. Turns out your boy Dylan Solly's sweet on Shinsuke's girl, least that's my guess since they're travelling together. And that's where it gets complicated. She's seen me. My cover's blown. But maybe that don't matter now.'

Okada shrugged. 'No.'

'Look, I'm fixin' to wrap up this piece of business. I got other matters to deal with. So, before you chop off Shinsuke's leg, I got a couple of loose ends to tie up. One, what do you want me to do with lil' Kasper?' Shultz nodded towards Kasper's waxen form over on the table.

'If he dies, dispose of him,' Okada said. 'If he lives, kill him.'

'I always get the damn dirty work … that'll cost you extra. And the girl?'

'Where is she?'

'On her way to Cape Sōya with your target. That's where her mom lives these days.'

'Bring her to Shinsuke.'

'What about Solly?'

Okada picked up a crimson hacksaw. 'Leave him to me.'

FIFTY-FOUR

D ylan fashioned a knapsack from a blanket and Betty's broken mop handle. The old woman looked at his makeshift bag, shook her head and handed him a rucksack.

'And take this,' she said, passing him a piece of cardboard scrawled with Japanese words in a green marker pen. 'It says *Hello, I'm Dylan Solly from England. I'm going to Cape Sōya because I'm in love.* This will reassure people. Hold it up so I can see.'

He did, and she chewed her pen cap. 'I'll add that you can speak a little Japanese at the bottom.'

'That feels like over-egging the pudding,' Dylan said.

Betty shot him a look.

'I mean, it's an exaggeration.'

'Nonsense,' she said. She annotated her work and translated for him – *Sorry to bother you* at the top, and *Thank you* below.

'Perfect. Now smile.'

She waved Mika over and took their picture with a disposable camera. Dylan blinked as the flash flared.

'Perfect,' Betty said. 'The happy couple.'

'Remember, English,' Betty said, leaning out of the window, 'if you see Buddha on the road, kill him. Good luck!' She laughed and drove off.

Mika led Dylan to Odori Park. Glass buildings fenced in a slip of snow-patched land sandwiched between busy carriageways.

'Every February, Sapporo hosts its seven-day winter festival here,' Mika said. 'The town gathers to create sculptures out of the fresh snow. Imagine it. Some of them are forty foot high. Even the army joins in.'

'It sounds like an old hippy's dream,' Dylan said. 'I love the idea of soldiers putting down guns and picking up snow trowels.'

At the far end, they came to a busy intersection where professionals carrying newspapers and briefcases crossed over to a high street packed with big-brand shops. Dylan and Mika stopped on the verge and watched the horde pass them.

'Look at those folks,' Dylan said. 'They're all in a hurry. They all have somewhere to be.' He put an arm around Mika. 'But not you and me. You know, not having a deadline for once feels kind of good. Even though I'm in a country I can't navigate on my own, I feel free.'

Sapporo's commuter-hour buzz reminded Dylan of Manchester – another vibrant city full of busy people who seemed to be in competition with each other. At least his career as journalist–adventurer hadn't required him to wear a suit. Those were for funerals and the occasional award ceremony.

They joined the crowd on the high street. 'I've no idea what a nine-to-five routine's like,' he said. 'All that stress, Monday to Friday.'

'It's not stressful if you enjoy your job,' Mika said.

'I wonder what that's like. I've only ever known the bullshit that comes from grinding out a career. I wonder how many people actually get a kick out of what they do.'

'These people are trying to make something of themselves,' Mika said, grabbing his arm as the tide of people threatened to separate them. 'They're aiming for the top, trying to be respectable. Judging and whining about it's no good for anyone. They're trying to be a light rather than a blight on the world.'

Dylan shrugged. 'Seems like they're trapped to me. Commuter traffic, stupid office meetings, more commuter traffic … and when they finally get home they're fucked. The highlight of their day is watching television and—'

'Your glass is always half empty, isn't it? And mind your language, Dylan Solly.'

'Sorry, but there's nothing for me in this city, or any other. Apart from you.'

Mika rolled her eyes.

It took only ten minutes for Betty's sign to work its magic. A massive blue Toyota Hilux pickup with impressively lumpy tyres pulled up, and Dylan introduced himself and asked the driver to take them to Cape Sōya. He understood only half the driver's reply.

'Perfect,' Mika said, and jumped into the back seat.

FIFTY-FIVE

Shultz looked over at the single-storey cabin where Opere Ito lived, and blew cigarette smoke out of the car window.

'Mother's in the kitchen,' he said into his phone. 'The cat's not in the cradle. Repeat – *not* in the cradle. I'll check back in an hour.'

He drove to the cliff edge of a coastal dirt road and dragged the blanket-wrapped cargo out from the boot. Waves crashed against the rocks and birds called out in the air above.

'Good a place as any, buddy,' he said. 'See you on the other side, Kasper the Friendly Ghost.'

He pushed the corpse over the edge and down into the seething ocean. A second, smaller parcel followed. After that, he flicked the dead butt of his cigarette into the foaming sea too. 'Your buddy Dylan will be joining you real soon.'

FIFTY-SIX

The drive north took them six hours. Chou dropped them off in Rumoi, a sparse coastal village decorated with colourful, weather-worn timber houses. To the side of the unpaved road stood an old minshuku – a family-run bed and breakfast.

'How far is it to Cape Sōya?' Dylan asked.

'Two hours,' Chou said. 'A hundred and fifty kilometres.'

'Hear that, Mika? You're nearly home.'

'This is the only landmark around here,' Chou said, pointing to the B&B's pink exterior. 'This village is pretty rural. You might have to wait a while before you see another car. Sorry I can't take you further but I'm heading on to Fukagawa, then back to Sapporo.'

'This will do fine. Thank you,' Mika said.

Chou wished them luck and drove off, rear tyres spitting dirt.

'It's beautiful,' Dylan said. Finally, he felt relaxed and his head had stopped throbbing. A breeze teased the branches of the many broad-leaved trees.

'Look!' Mika pointed beyond the minshuku. 'The ocean! Let's go.'

The water looked calm and tempting. Despite feeling battered and weary, Dylan couldn't resist.

A narrow track between rice fields led them to the glittering sea with a single ship on the horizon. Birds hovered above the dark sands. Mika was soon naked and splashing in the midday tide. Dylan joined her, wearing nothing but the chain around his neck. They embraced.

'I love the way you flicker your eyelashes and smile,' he said.

'I don't *flicker* my eyes.' She laughed and batted her lashes. 'At least I don't think I do.'

'Whatever it is, I like it.'

Mika shook her head.

'What's up?' Dylan said.

'For the first time in my life I feel … free. But I've been unlucky in love before. I'm scared. It feels like we're living in a daydream.'

He felt the same. And even if this was real life now, how long could it last?

FIFTY-SEVEN

An hour passed in a blink. Mika and Dylan left the beach and returned to the small pink minshuku. After forty-five minutes of holding Betty's cardboard sign and getting nowhere, Mika decided they needed another plan.

'I'll ask the owner how to get to the next village. It's a nice day for a walk, and it can't be that far. Are you feeling strong enough to hike? I'll carry the bag.'

Dylan handed over the rucksack. 'I'm fine when I'm upright and moving. The swim helped. Let's give it a try.'

They were given directions to Usuya, a tiny town forty kilometres north of Rumoi. White waves just crested the edge of coastal highway 239, so they walked along the grassy embankment on the other side of the road. As the afternoon warmed, they stopped regularly, taking advantage of shade. Once they picnicked on a verdant hill, and a family of tiny-eared rabbits sunned themselves as Mika and Dylan ate. A light breeze rippled the grass.

Mika continued with her Japanese lessons as they passed Usuya and trekked on to Obira. At each town, they consulted shopkeepers on the best route north. Some marvelled at meeting a foreigner, others were charmed by Mika. All were helpful but none could offer them a ride.

Soon Tomamae was in their sights. They crossed a bridge, went through a tunnel, and came out into a pastel-pink sky. The sun set, the temperature dropped, and the stars came out. Mika and Dylan unrolled their blankets and lay down on a grassy bank overlooking the ocean.

Neither spoke. Mika's head rested in the crook of Dylan's neck. He inhaled the scent of her hair teasing his chin, felt the warmth of her body against his, and wondered if this was love.

A restaurant owner took pity on them. It was a small outlet at the edge of Tomamae, a narrow wooden room with a low ceiling, but what it lacked in space it made up for in organisation and hospitality. The proprietor – too tall for the premises – gave them coffee and let them stock their rucksack with yesterday's fruit and vegetables. They told him their story while he crouched open-mouthed at their table, then insisted they take more food and water and bagged up additional supplies at the counter.

'If you sleep outside at night,' he said, 'take care you don't get hypothermia. And even on cloudy days in March you can get sunburned. And don't stray too far from the roads, the terrain can be hazardous. I have a shower upstairs –you're welcome to use it.'

Dylan felt healthy and free. Mika seemed jittery and unsteady on her feet.

Dylan decided to chance his arm. 'Is there any possibility you could drive us to the next village?'

'I'm sorry, I only have a Super Cub.' The owner pointed to the window. A small red and white motorcycle rested against the glass. 'There's only room on the back for one.'

'How about it, Mika?' Dylan said, 'You go. I'll meet you in Cape Sōya.'

She screwed up her face. 'It's a beautiful morning. Let's carry on walking.'

They ignored their host's advice and left the road, instead strolling across the open land that swept along the coast under a clear cyan sky. The sea frothed and thrashed, and gulls swooped above their heads. To their right, woodland protected them from the rest of the world. They were alone. Not another soul.

The long walk wasn't easy, but Dylan felt driven, that what he was doing was right, that he'd finally found the right path, one that had long been hidden but was now clearly marked by Mika's footsteps.

He teased the ring on his necklace. *Eden all over again.*

'Wait,' he said, and stopped.

'What is it?' Mika said.

'These past few days, we've been through everything. Terrible events. We've witnessed death and escaped it, though we didn't come away unscathed. I wouldn't have made it without you. I've seen the world, the good and the bad, but I've never been more at peace than right now. I'm battered and bruised and a million miles from home, but I feel amazing, and I owe it all to you. I'd have worked myself to death if we hadn't met. You're the most incredible person I've ever met.'

He dropped onto one knee, took the chain from his neck and released the ring. 'Like a dandelion gives its body to the wind, I give myself to you, Mika Ito. Will you marry me?'

Mika put a hand to her mouth. Stepped back.

And replied with a single word.

FIFTY-EIGHT

'No.'

Dylan stayed kneeling, holding out the battered old ring as the ocean breeze picked up. 'What?'

Mika turned away. 'I can't.'

'Can't or won't? "No" is fine, but why?'

'My father won't allow it.'

'I'll ask him for your hand in marriage, like Betty said. He'll come around once I talk to him.'

His knee complained as he stood but he ignored the pain and tried to pull Mika close. She held back, and a tear rolled down her cheek.

'I think I love you, Dylan, but we can't. Anytime I've felt this way, bad things happen. It's not safe.'

'Don't be crazy.'

'I should have told you, but I didn't know how ...' She took a breath. 'My father ... my father is Shinsuke Takahashi, the Tomioka Torturer, and he's killed every man I have ever loved.'

For a moment, her words tumbled together. This made no sense. It couldn't be true.

'You didn't think to mention this? I talked about him enough!'

'How could I? How would anyone bring such a thing into conversation? Besides, you'd have just wanted to make it into one of your articles.' Mika's eyes blazed. 'And what business is it of yours or anyone else? I have to be somebody's daughter. What should I do? Introduce myself appropriately? Hi, I'm Mika, the estranged daughter of a serial killer.'

'You should have—'

'He's not the man I knew! I haven't seen or heard from him in seven years, and I didn't know who he was until my mother told me after Hiro died. You don't know what it's like. Every day I have to put on armour and pretend I'm not his daughter. I want a simple life, Dylan, that's all. No more heartache, no more pain. And I still can't figure it out. My papa was a good man. He walked me to school every day.' Her tears fell fast over her anger. 'He loved baseball and karaoke and barbecues and trips to the park. I don't know the Tomioka Torturer, I only know my papa, and I don't understand what happened to him. It wasn't my papa who kidnapped Ken when I was fourteen and killed Riku and took Hiro from me—'

'Mika.'

'What?'

'Your father is dead. On the night of the tsunami, I saw him buried under wreckage.'

'Dead?' Her voice was barely a whisper above the breeze.

'I can't be one hundred per cent certain, but he was dying, I'm sure.'

She pulled at her hair. 'You left my papa to die?'

'He's better off dead – he was a monster. You just said it yourself.'

'That monster was my father.'

He reached for her but she refused his embrace.

'You kill my father then ask me to marry you?'

She stared at him, shook her head, then ran.

He limped after her. 'That's not how this is,' he called out. 'How could I have known? You can't run from this your whole life. Talk to me!'

Mika sprinted into the bushes. Dylan lumbered after her, calling her name, desperate now. But she was gone.

FIFTY-NINE

M ika charged through the thicket, leaves smacking against her face, branches and twigs clawing at her arms. She looked left, then right as she ran, but it all looked the same. Her foot caught and she tripped, tried to right herself and stumbled forward, sliding over loose soil. Then she was tumbling through a blur of green and brown, until something hard slammed into her body, breaking her fall ...

She came to, opened her eyes, and pulled herself up to a sitting position. Her muscles protested and pain fired through her shoulders. Night had set in but the moonlit sky was bright, revealing her tumultuous path down the ravine. Leaves and cold dirt covered her body.

So she'd fallen. It was dark. She was injured. And tired, so very, very tired. She lay back, rolled onto her side and fell asleep.

A cawing woke her. A crow perhaps. Night had turned to day but the pain was just the same. Her face felt tight, and she rubbed at it and looked at her hands. Her fingers were smeared with dried blood.

Where the hell was she? Where had she been going? *Think.*

She crawled forward a couple of feet and using a tree trunk as leverage, hauled herself onto her feet.

There was a rucksack on her back. She eased it off her shoulders and rummaged inside. A battered cardboard sign in a script she didn't recognise read: *Sorry to bother you. I'm Dylan Solly from England. I'm going to Cape Sōya because I'm in love. I can speak a little Japanese. Thank you.*

Who was Dylan Solly?

Her head hurt and she was ravenously hungry. Every moment felt new and slow.

There was more in the backpack – squashed fruit and vegetables, which she devoured, and painkillers. Water too. She swallowed the pills and read the sign again, hoping to stoke a fire of recognition. It still made no sense. She needed help. Maybe she'd find it at Cape Sōya, wherever that was.

She picked a direction and resigned herself to the painful task of walking.

SIXTY

A man – young, slight, local – was leading a herd of cows through a field in the valley. Mika showed him the cardboard sign. He pointed to the fields ahead and broke the bad news to her. Cape Sōya was far away, very far away. He offered her water, and although there was still some in her bag, she drank half of what he had. He looked bamboozled and wished her good luck.

She took a twisting road that led her upwards. Something struck the back of her head and she turned sharply. Nothing but empty land surrounded her. She looked up. A bird with black feathers swooped and dived towards her. She ducked and the crow flew off, victorious.

The pain was the only constant. Everything else was a blur, like she'd just emerged from sleep. She stopped to catch her breath, and a memory blinked in her mind: in bed, Papa tucking her in. Her staring at a ceiling, worried about an upcoming English exam, unable to sleep.

When was that? Where was Papa? What about Mom?

She continued to walk. Beyond were dense smokestacks, antennas and grey buildings. Later, she stumbled onto a rocky beach littered with white polythene bags, plastic yellow bottles, rubber tyres, smashed glass and seaweed. A rusty push bike was half-buried in the pebbles exposed by the low tide.

She found the road again. The light faded, giving way to an inky-blue evening. A large coal truck blew past her and threw loose pebbles in its wake.

Better to stay off the road.

She lay down on a patch of grass and closed her eyes.

Mika woke sometime later, stressed about a language exam. Then the rain came and a million crisp white explosions bounced off the tarmac and over her body, soaking her. She shivered as the cold water dripped over her eyebrows and poured down her face.

She got up, and stumbled onward until she came to a bus stop offering merciful shelter. The rain pounded against the metal roof, and the panic she'd been trying to supress found its legs.

What was she doing here?

The walls of the small wooden shed were plastered with posters advertising local funeral services and employment opportunities in the military. She tried to decipher the timetable and checked her bag for money.

She had none. No food either.

She'd wait anyway.

Up ahead, just before a bend in the road, was a worn-out billboard advertising a doctor's surgery.

Papa …

Her hand in his during the walk to school. His voice as he asked her about her day. Memories of barbecues and baseball games surfaced, then disappeared just as quickly.

The rain stopped. No bus came, so she walked on in search of somebody, anybody. The day warmed, and when the relentless heat and the glare of the sun became too much, and insect bites had mottled the skin on her arms, she hid in the cleft of a rock face and shaded her eyes as she munched on painkillers.

She'd lost the road but wasn't sure how, or when. In the distance, a snow-capped mountain loomed over a body of water. Its silvery peak offered a sense of direction. As for her sore shoulders, tired legs, the cryptic handwritten sign – they were her only psychic anchors. Everything else had a question mark attached to it.

Her lips cracked, her ankles swelled, hunger gnawed at her belly. Cantankerous, bare-branched trees taunted her. A blood-red sun laughed in a pale-razor sky. Then came the visions – of boiling bones and showers of salt. She prayed for summer rain as she stared at her blistered heels and bruised toes.

Keep going. Keep going.

Cape Sōya. She had to get to Cape Sōya.

Every patch of shadow was life. Relief for her scorched skin. Breaking down the dirt-road journey, little by little, brought her closer to a narrow tunnel of peace.

I'm killing Buddha with every step. Killing Buddha …

Where had that come from?

Then there were people – a man and a young girl up ahead, walking hand in hand. Mika called out, waved, and ran to them.

The girl turned and smiled.

Blood dripped from the hand she was holding.

The hand belonged to Papa. The girl was a young Mika.

Memories fell like bombs.

Shinsuke Takahashi charged towards her.

'Please, Papa! No!'

A deafening roar engulfed her, and a blizzard of dust swept over the mirage and dissolved. And there, in the road, was a red and white motorcycle.

SIXTY-ONE

Opere peered over an easel at a pygmy woodpecker perched on a branch, and brushed a soft brown line onto the canvas. Her porch had always been the best place to observe birds sunning themselves in the early evening. The woodpecker twitched and flew from the tree as a motorbike sped towards the gate, kicking dust into the air.

She picked up her shotgun and trained it on the rider.

'Ms Ito! My name is Dylan Solly. Mika needs your help!'

Mika lay on the couch, Dylan's hand stroking hers.

'You spoke to my mom in Japanese,' she said. 'I'm so proud of you.'

'I have a good teacher. I thought you were gone, Mika. I searched everywhere but you'd just disappeared. I panicked and went back to the restaurant. The owner leant me his bike. I must have covered every road between Cape Sōya and Tomamae.'

Opere handed Mika a cup of tea. 'My poor girl, you look so frail. Drink this, it'll warm you up.'

The doctor checked Mika over and took a blood sample, then packed up his case, saying he'd check back on her progress in a few days. 'Rest, fluids, food, and love, that's my prescription. And I'm sure Mother Ito can help with those.' He bowed to Opere. 'As for your male guest, Ms Ito, I can certainly—'

'That'll be all, doctor,' Opere said.

The doctor smiled, bowed once more and left.

'Mika, you must be starved,' her mother said, and stroked Mika's muddied hair.

Opere retreated to the kitchen, and Mika said, 'I've been thinking. We haven't been together for very long and there's so much I don't know about you. I see so many challenges in our future. Where will you live? How will you find work? Will you get a permanent visa? And what if my father *is* alive? I didn't realise how scared I am of him. Being with you seems so dangerous, but being without you it feels impossible. When we're together, the other stuff disappears.' She sat up. 'Ask me again.'

'What?'

'Ask me again. Quick.' She glanced at the kitchen door.

Dylan dropped onto one knee and produced his ring. 'Mika Ito, you're funny, you're cute, and you're a very difficult woman to find after an argument. Will you marry me?'

She put a finger to her lips, then whispered, 'Yes.'

He placed the battered bronze ring on her finger. 'I can't say things will be easy, and I don't have all the answers.'

'Just promise me we'll be okay.'

The ring was oversized and felt heavy on her finger.

'It's a perfect fit,' she lied. 'I'll have to hide it till my mom knows.'

'I don't think your mum likes me. She hasn't said a word to me since we arrived, and it's not like I haven't tried. I've used up all my best Japanese. But she stares right through me. She even pointed a gun at me.'

'She's a grumpy, retired English teacher who's been through a lot since the divorce. Be gentle with her. She needs to get to know you, that's all. You should spend time with her. When the time's right, you can tell her.' Mika paused. 'Tomorrow morning, I'll arrange for you to go with her and see the red-crowned cranes at sunrise. She always talks about them, and they're not far from here. The western lakes – it's the most beautiful place. She loves those birds and she won't be grumpy around them. And you'll get to enjoy some nature while I have a well-deserved lie-in. Oh, and you can bring me breakfast from the village on your way back.'

'Sounds like a plan.'

The house was a small, open-plan, single-storey cabin in the wilderness. Mika had always thought it was the perfect place to hide away from the rest of the world. The kitchen was in a newer extension at the back, through a tiny door. The older living room was heated by an open fire. Its walls were dotted with square sepia photographs of women with tattooed mouths.

Dylan went over to one and peered at it.

'That's an old Ainu tradition,' Mika said. 'They were the indigenous people of Hokkaido. My ancestors. The old ways are gone now. Their language was banned and their land taken.'

Dylan pointed to a short-barrelled shotgun propped up against the wall by the door. The firearm had seen better days.

'Looks like something out of a Western,' Dylan said. 'What's it for?'

'I don't know. Bears?'

Opere returned with a tray of food. She handed it to Mika and kissed her on the cheek. 'Is it warm enough in here for you?'

'Do you have a problem with bears around here, Ms Ito?' Dylan said.

Opere stoked the fire. 'The only problem I have here is with intruders.'

SIXTY-TWO

At 5 a.m. on the dot, Dylan tiptoed out of the cabin behind a well-insulated Opere. A thin frost covered everything, and he regretted not having a coat. They marched through the inky pre-morning light over rough terrain, and after what seemed like miles, dawn broke and they entered woodland.

Neither had spoken a word.

Dylan was struggling to keep pace. His head throbbed, his ribs ached, and a change of head dressing was overdue. And he was hungry. 'This is quite a hike,' he said.

Still Opere said nothing, just marched onward.

Ten minutes later, and to Dylan's relief, they stopped in a clearing. The view took his breath away. Fifty or so cranes were drinking from a series of small lakes. But for the black secondary feathers on their wings and necks, and the ruby-red crowns they'd been named for, the birds were snow white.

'They're incredible,' he said, feeling the chill in his bones. 'Thank you for bringing me out here. I can see why this place is so special to you. We should invite Mika next time. I know she'd enjoy it.' He cleared his throat. 'Speaking of Mika, I'm glad we have this chance to talk because—'

'Look at how majestic they are,' Opere said just behind him. 'Go on, look. Look.'

Two of the cranes began to dance with a bold, playful show of their wings.

'These birds mate for life,' she whispered. 'Imagine that, finding a partner to share your whole life with, side by side, forever. Isn't it wonderful? But it's not always that way for us, as I've found to my cost. I've learned that some relationships are just not meant to be, while others simply *cannot* be.'

Dylan watched Opere's shadow move across the grass in front of him. She was reaching into her coat, pulling something out.

He recognised the shape.

A shotgun.

Cold metal pressed against the back of his head.

'I'll give you one chance,' Opere said. 'One chance to get away from my daughter.'

SIXTY-THREE

Dylan turned, grabbed the barrel, and pushed it away. 'What the hell are you doing?'

'I'm trying to help you!' Opere pulled the heavy wooden stock towards her.

Dylan tightened his grip and wrestled the gun from her. Too easy, even with his injuries.

She crumpled to the floor and he turned the gun on her.

'What the hell's wrong with you?'

Her face softened, and her strength seemed to vanish on the mist of her breath.

'You'll never understand,' she said, her voice barely audible.

'*You* killed her lovers, didn't you?'

Opere stared out at the lakes and the dancing cranes.

'Answer me!'

She grabbed the muzzle and held it against her chest. 'You might as well pull the trigger, but promise me you'll leave Mika and get away from this place. Listen to me – her father's going to kill you.'

'Her father's dead.'

'No, he isn't. He sent people to watch the house. Shinsuke Taka-hashi is capable of unspeakable things, and he's coming for you. You have to get out of here.'

Dylan lowered the gun and handed it back to Opere. 'No. He

won't. Because you're going to help me stop him.'

'I've tried and failed.' She looked again towards the mirrored surfaces of the lakes and sighed. 'This started so long ago ... with her first boyfriend, Ken. He was fourteen and such a polite young man. He had his whole life ahead of him, but Shinsuke couldn't stand him. That was the first time I saw my husband's temper.' She took off her coat and put it around Dylan. 'Ken disappeared. His body was eventually found. He'd been beaten and burned. It shocked the whole town, and Mika was so upset ... I never thought she'd get over it. I never suspected my husband, had no idea he was capable of murder. I thought I was happily married to a doctor.

'Then Mika met Riku when she was sixteen. I was relieved because it meant she was ready to try again. Riku was charming, but Shinsuke was furious when he found out. One day, Riku called the house and Shinsuke answered. I didn't recognise my husband – he said such terrible things to that poor boy. A dog walker found Riku's body in the woods three weeks later. It worried me but I couldn't believe my husband – a doctor, a good man – was responsible.

'Three years later, Mika grew close to a teacher at the school – Hiro. After only a few months, she was planning a whole life with him. And she was happy. A month later, he was found dead – beaten and burned, just like Ken and Riku. Then I knew. It had to be Shinsuke. I was devastated but I called the police. They thought I was crazy. And maybe I was – after all, I was living with a madman. So I ran away, and now I'm here on the edge of the world.'

Dylan shook his head. 'I was going to ask him for Mika's hand in marriage.'

'That would be suicide.' She sat on the trunk of a felled tree and cradled her gun. 'Ever since his sister passed, he's been ... different.' She wiped her cheek. 'I can still remember her funeral well. Why are the painful memories always the strongest? Sara was her name. She left us too soon. I can't believe it's been thirteen years?'

'How did she die?' Dylan asked.

'Huntington's disease. There's no cure and her symptoms just got worse. But she was strong and we loved her. Our marriage was good then. Until the morning Shinsuke found Sara in tears. Her husband had left her, packed up and gone because he couldn't bear to watch her deteriorating. That hurt Sara deep in her soul.'

Opere said a silent prayer into her hands. 'No matter what we tried, we couldn't get her to talk, eat, drink even. Shinsuke stayed by Sara's side until the end. He stayed up all night crying. She'd died broken-hearted, he said. And that's why he can't let go of Mika.'

'What do you mean?'

'Mika has Huntington's too, though we haven't told her. And the way Shinsuke sees it, every man who Mika falls in love with is just another man who'll do to her what was done to his sister. The idea of that haunts him.'

Dylan rubbed his temples, absorbing the bombshell Opere had just dropped. 'Are you sure Mika has it?'

'Yes. She was tested when she was young. She might live a long life or she might not. So be honest with yourself – will you still love her when she becomes ill? When she can't speak or eat or swallow? When she's angry and stubborn and needs care around the clock? You hardly know her. Leave her. Save her from dying with a broken heart. And save yourself.'

Dylan let her words sink in for a moment, then said, 'She's a grown woman. You have to tell her.'

'I wanted to when she was a teenager, but Shinsuke would say, "You're just a housewife. What do you know?" I was tired of the arguments so I deferred to him. All I've ever wanted is for Mika to be happy and live without a shadow over her future. Maybe keeping it a secret was wrong. I didn't say it was a perfect decision. I can't say I'm an example for other parents to follow, but I've never wanted to be an example. I've only ever wanted to be a good mother.'

'Then talk to her.' Dylan handed Opere her coat. 'She's stronger than you think.'

SIXTY-FOUR

Opere suggested they pick up fresh grilled fish from the village. Dylan offered no protest; it would give him space to think.

The takeaway bag was still warm when they arrived back at the cottage. He was about to call out to Mika, tell her they had breakfast, but he froze at the door.

It was open.

And it shouldn't have been.

He ran in to the living room. The couch was on its back, the lamp smashed, the phone bouncing on its cord, beeping.

'Mika?'

Opere lifted the shotgun, and Dylan charged through to Mika's bedroom. Empty. Just an unmade bed.

He called her name again, and Opere pushed a finger to her lips and gestured towards the kitchen.

Dylan picked up a poker from the fireplace and pushed the door open. Also empty.

The back door hung off its hinges, its frame splintered. He ran out to the porch.

Still no sign of her.

The flower bed had been trampled over. Birds scattered. Something moved behind the maple tree at the end of the garden, and Dylan sprinted over to it.

Something slammed into him and he fell, his wrists jarring on the hard ground. He lost his grip on the poker, which bounced to the side, then scrambled onto his knees. A boot connected with his belly, knocking the air out of him.

Breathe.

He looked up. A figure loomed over him

Freddie Yoka.

'You skinny bitch. You ruined my tattoos.'

A hand grabbed Dylan's hair and pulled him up.

'Remember me, Mr Dylan Solly of England?'

Jushin Okada.

He threw Dylan's wallet at him. 'You should be more careful about what you leave lying around after a knife fight. Especially after what you did to Freddie.'

He slapped Dylan hard.

Dylan slipped, fell, staggered back to his knees. 'Where's Mika?'

A fist smacked him back down.

'Where she belongs,' Okada said. 'With her father. He wishes he could be here in person, but he's healing right now. Don't worry though, you're going to meet him very soon.'

'But first,' Yoka said, 'I want some fun.'

Yoka stepped back, lifted his leg, winding up for a strike.

The air cracked, and a red stain spread across his chest. He looked down, then crumpled to the ground. 'I've been shot! Some bastard shot me.'

Opere stood by the maple tree, smoke dancing from her gun.

'Get away from my son-in-law, you son of a bitch.'

Okada raised his hands. 'Of course, Ms Ito. Just put down the gun.'

'I'm losing blood. I think I'm dying,' Yoka moaned.

'I'll just help Mr Solly to his feet,' Okada said. No harm, no foul.'

He leaned down.

His hand shot to his ankle, and he pulled a pistol from the hidden holster.

'Kill him,' Yoka screamed. 'And kill that bitch.'

'Sorry, Ms Ito. Your houseguest and I have business to attend to. Now, I don't want to hurt you, out of respect for your husband, but if I need to, I will shoot you.'

'I don't have a husband,' Opere hissed, 'and I don't need scum on my property.'

Sirens wailed in the distance.

'I guess it's too late to be Mr Nice Guy,' Okada said.

As Okada squeezed the trigger, Dylan launched himself forward.

His shoulder connected with Okada's knee, and the Merchant lost his footing. The bullet went wide, splintering the bark of the tree, and the pistol spun over the ground.

Dylan gouged at the earth, trying to get a purchase and pull himself towards the firearm, but paw-like hands found his throat and began to crush his airway.

The sirens were close. Engines roared, then stopped. Doors slammed.

The pressure on Dylan's throat eased, and he heaved in blessed oxygen. 'Where's Mika?' he croaked.

Okada just laughed as the police dragged him away.

SIXTY-FIVE

The Hokkaido Herald, 23 March 2011

CELEBRATION AS TWO OF THREE RECAPTURED

The Japanese prime minister has praised Cape Sōya's small but mighty police force after the successful recapture of Freddie Yoka and Jushin Okada. The men make up two thirds of the Notorious Three, a criminal enterprise rumoured to be headquartered in Tomioka. The three men had escaped twelve days earlier during the unprecedented events of 11 March.

Jushin Okada is being transported to Tokyo, where he will be put before a judge at the earliest possible opportunity. Freddie Yoka was pronounced dead at the scene by paramedics. The cause of Mr Yoka's death is not yet clear. After yesterday's heroics by the police, only the leader Shinsuke Takahashi remains at large.

Prime Minister Suga has singled out the rural town's

Superintendent Usami for particular bravery, saying the officer has 'brought something positive to a nation in mourning'.

Said Superintendent Usami, 'As soon as I arrived at the scene, I knew we had a serious problem, but my training and skill guided me to make the most important arrest in Japan's history. It is an honour to serve my community. I am very happy.'

Several government officials on all sides of parliament have requested that Mr Usami be promoted to assistant commissioner in the wake of yesterday's dramatic events.

When *The Herald* asked about the cause of Mr Yoka's death, Superintendent Usami declined to comment, saying only that it is part of an ongoing investigation, and if any wrongdoing is discovered in the course of their enquiries, justice will be done.

SIXTY-SIX

Everything was wrong, the day a contradiction, a lie. How could the sun shine so bright, the breeze be so gentle, the sky bloom with magnificent pinks and yellows, the birds sing so merrily in high, unseen places? Where was the desert, the storms, the thunderclaps and ice sheets, the rise and fall of time? Where were those things now that she was gone?

Dylan perched on the edge of Opere's couch and reached for the ring at his neck. Its absence stung.

He called *Topic International*, hoping to reach Violet again. A sleepy-sounding voice announced he'd reached someone called Joe. Dylan introduced himself as Bobby Dibs – the name of his old flat-mate – and asked after Violet. Her contract had been 'released' apparently, but Joe sounded half asleep and clearly hadn't been briefed on the company's privacy policy. He told Dylan to wait while he spoke to HR, and three minutes later, Dylan had Violet's personal number.

He called her.

'I stole Sam's recorder!' she squeaked. 'And I'm glad I did. You wouldn't believe the things I've heard. I've been taking notes nonstop for days. This could be a huge story. In fact, it might be *several* massive stories. I'll email—'

'Violet, I do want to get to that, but I've got bigger fish to fry right now and I need your help. I'm in Japan and I'm shit out of luck. I've no money, no passport. Please listen. I just got engaged to Shinsuke Takahashi's daughter – and now she's been kidnapped by her father. I've no idea where she is, and I don't know where to start looking.'

The line went quiet.

'Violet?'

'Sorry, that's a lot to unpack. Have you contacted the police?'

Dylan tossed the copy of *The Hokkaido Herald* to the end of the sofa.

'The police have no leads. It's been over twenty-four hours and all they've done is take a witness account, file a missing person's report, and claim a whole lot of glory for arresting Jushin Okada. The cops are just happy to have apprehended two of the Notorious Three. Case closed. Time to celebrate as far as they're concerned. There isn't a word about Mika – the police just give us the same old bollocks every time we call. She's in danger, Violet. Her father's a maniac, totally unhinged. I wouldn't put it past him to force her into that small torture box of his or—'

'Dylan, slow down. I'd like to help, but how?'

'I honestly don't know. I'll be in touch. And, Violet, thanks for listening.'

SIXTY-SEVEN

He couldn't sleep, just sat in the kitchen, staring at the patched-up door and police tape.

Above the hiss of the steaming tea kettle, there came a light tap at the front door. Mika? Was she back?

He opened the door. No one there. Just the cool air and starlight.

And in the middle of the wooden deck a small, unmarked box.

He took it into the kitchen, peeled back the tape and opened it. Inside, were a smattering of pink blossoms and the rumpled pages from yesterday's newspaper.

Stained with blood.

He unfurled the paper, revealing their contents.

And collapsed.

Superintendent Usami produced a pad from his pocket, then brushed his dark hair out his eyes for the umpteenth time. He wore a long coat, flat-soled shoes and creased slacks.

'Can anyone vouch for your whereabouts last night, Mr Solly?'

Opere served tea.

'Thank you, ma'am. Perhaps you can help. Mr Solly doesn't seem very responsive.'

'I'm afraid his grasp of Japanese isn't perfect, and he's in shock.'

'I understand, I do. A terrible thing – what he found in that box. Did you see it yourself?'

How would she ever unsee it? The clotted stump of the severed finger ... the blood-smeared bronze ring attached to it.

What was Mika enduring at the hands of her ex-husband? She swallowed hard. 'I'm afraid I did.'

'You seem to be handling it much better than Mr Solly. Can anyone vouch for your whereabouts yesterday evening?'

'Only Dylan.'

'I see ... interesting. And you and Mika are on good terms?'

'I love my daughter.'

'I see. Ms Ito – may I call you Ms Ito?'

She nodded.

Usami checked his notebook and enquired nervously, 'Forgive me if I'm wrong, but you aren't the same woman who shot a man dead in your garden in the early hours of yesterday morning?'

'Correct.'

The superintendent made a note. 'This might be a sensitive question, but I have to ask these things – it's standard police procedure, you understand. If I don't ask, my boss will send me right back. He's a tough nut. So, if you'll allow me, what kind of relationship does Mr Solly have with your daughter?'

'They're engaged.'

'Has he ever been abusive, ever raised a hand to her?'

'No, Mr Usami—'

'Superintendent.'

'Of course. Superintendent Usami, Mika was kidnapped by her father, Shinsuke Takahashi.'

Usami drew a breath. 'Yes, you mentioned that name earlier. Unfortunately, there have been no reports about his whereabouts. Would you happen to know where he is?'

'Of course not.'

'I see. Tell me, how long were you married to the Tomioka Torturer?'

'Twenty years.'

'Can I ask what kind of woman could marry a man like that?'

Opere set down her cup. 'Superintendent Usami, if you're not going to say or do anything meaningful, drink your tea and leave.'

He pushed at his hair again. 'Well, I think I have everything I need. I'll write a report and get back to you.' He pocketed his notebook and looked at Dylan. 'You should get him to hospital or some other place of healing. Thank you again, Ms Ito.'

The superintendent slammed the door on his way out.

Dylan, his complexion grey, stared at a single blood-stained blossom, just liked he'd been doing all morning.

'What did he say?'

'That we should send you to a hospital. He's such a stupid man.'

'He mentioned another place.'

'A place of healing.'

Dylan muttered the words several times. 'I've heard that before.'

'You must eat, Dylan. Let me make you something.'

'Shinsuke was a doctor, wasn't he?'

'He was. But even if you could find him, I hardly think he's the man to go to for medical attention.'

'And Jushin Okada said he was healing somewhere, presumably recovering from the night of the tsunami. He can't go to a hospital; he's a wanted man. Where would he go?'

'He used to work at a medical practice.'

Dylan rubbed his temples. 'But this blossom ... he once told Mika there was only one real place of healing.'

'You don't think—'

'I do.'

Dylan bolted from the couch and ran outside. Opere heard the whine of an engine, stumbled over to the door, and watched the little red and white Super Cub motorcycle speed away.

SIXTY-EIGHT

It was noon when Dylan arrived at the graveyard that was once a thriving coastal village. Tomioka was eerily calm, its crooked and splintered buildings like sharp, broken teeth surrounded by sentinels – toppled boats, crushed cars, wrecked timber. He cruised through the park towards the shell of Mika's apartment and his mind reconstructed Tomioka, one piece at a time, until every violent moment since 11th March appeared in the shadows of the late-morning star.

Hold on, Mika. Hold on.

The military relief effort hadn't made it this far east, not since the evacuation order had come in. Tomioka was too close to the Fukushima fallout zone for a rescue mission. The whole place was a risk to life, and the village and its surrounds for miles beyond had been declared a no-go zone.

It was here that Dylan readied himself to meet his nemesis.

The Tomioka Torturer.

He passed the school, still stained by the high-water mark. He peered through the window at damaged posters and decaying furniture piled up in corners.

But he'd not find her here.

Nor could his borrowed bike take him all the way. The last mile would have to be completed on foot.

The shattered road trailed off to a small footpath, the passage he and Mika had walked on the fateful night of a new quarter moon.

Chest throbbing with adrenaline, he neared the pink cherry blossom trees that surrounded the small Shinto shrine on the hill. He paused at the torii gate and paid his respects to the guardian deities. The red timber frame and sloping gabled roof seemed to welcome him, but the two stone lion dogs protecting the inner worship hall made the space feel like a fortress.

He stepped onto the sacred ground and washed his hands in the fountain, just as Mika had taught him.

The water had a reddish tinge to it.

A voice echoed across the courtyard, from beyond the moss-stained Komainu. It took the wind out of him.

'You're a difficult man to kill. You English are too stubborn to die. But I know your weakness, Dylan Solly.'

Dylan approached the temple's interior, bowed and entered the open hall. It was bright inside. Behind the paper doors at the far end of the room was the silhouette of a figure in a wheelchair.

'Dylan Solly, are you a warrior or an errand boy?'

The doors opened, revealing the unmistakable round glasses and long silver hair of the Tomioka Torturer.

One leg of his grey suit trousers was rolled up, exposing a heavily bandaged stump. Despite the recent trauma, Shinsuke Takahashi still had an ease about him.

'You've either come to fight an old man or ask him for his daughter's hand. Which is it, Mr Solly?'

'The latter.'

'A whole hand?' Takahashi tutted. 'I've already given you a finger. You Westerners are so greedy.'

'Where is she?'

'My daughter? This isn't about her. It's about you.'

'I don't speak Japanese very well, but you seem to understand me well enough, so listen. I'm not here to fight. Just please don't hurt Mika. Please let her go.'

'I'll say this in English so there can be no mistake. Mr Solly, there's a difference between you and me, it's why you'll never be good enough for my daughter. You see, I'm an assassin, a predator. I'll do anything to get what I want, and I'm prepared to destroy anybody who gets in my way. But you?' He smiled. 'When you pull up to a gas station and somebody jerks open your car door and says, "Get out. This car's mine now," you say, "Okay, take it. Just don't hurt me." You want to know what I do? I pull out my gun and spray his brains all over the tarmac. Because I'm Shinsuke Takahashi, and I'll be damned if I'm going to let a loser break my daughter's heart.'

'You mutilated your own daughter. If you love her, how can you be so cruel?'

'No, the world is cruel, not me. It's a terrible world, isn't it? Violent men doing violent things, always and till the end of time.'

'Is that your excuse for what you've done to Mika, for all the people you've killed?'

'How is it any different from what fishermen do to fish, farmers to cattle, motorists to the poor little animals that try and cross the road? No, the only difference is that I embrace what I do. I don't hide who I am. Governments destroy the planet, wipe out anything that gets in the way, and call it market forces. I call it what it is – *death*. We all tolerate murder whenever it suits us, so why cry for one life? Humanity is built on murder. There have been dead bodies on every road you've ever travelled. Tell me, Mr Innocent, how do you justify leaving me in the dark to die? You're no better than me.' Takahashi pointed at his chest. 'At least I accept what I am.'

'But what has Mika done—'

'It's all Mika, Mika, Mika with you. Look, if you hadn't met her, you'd be with be some other woman. And at this stage in her life, despite all that's gone into protecting her, we both know she's as good as dead. You see how she moves, see how she shakes. Time will not be kind to her. She's obsessed with love, but only because she doesn't know what comes after it. But I know what happens next – for her and you. I see your future. So, ask me. Come here and get on your knees and ask for permission to marry her.'

Dylan didn't move.

'Do it!'

'If I do, will you let Mika go?'

'Of course.' Takahashi put a hand on his heart. 'You have my word of honour.'

Dylan edged towards the wheelchair, desperate for an alternative but out of options. He put his head to the temple floor.

'Shinsuke Takahashi, may I marry your daughter?'

Takahashi's laugh was low and rough. 'Such a stupid boy. You should never have come here.'

Dylan peered up. The muzzle of a gun grazed his forehead. The old man smiled. 'Isn't it a pity.'

A boom split the air.

SIXTY-NINE

Opere's long overcoat swayed in the wind. Hot smoke spiralled from her shotgun.

'I see the lion dogs failed to keep away your evil spirit,' she said.

'If it isn't my good lady wife,' Takahashi said.

'Ex-wife.'

Dylan lunged towards Takahashi, but the old man smacked him across the head with the pistol, and he crashed to the floor. The room spun, time refused to tick. He staggered to his knees but Takahashi rapped him across the temple again, and Dylan collapsed back down to the ground. Warm blood trickled down his face.

'Leave him alone! He loves her, Shinsuke. Like you loved me once.'

'The world needs more than love.'

She aimed the shotgun, her eyes full of tears. 'The years have not been kind to you. You're just a bitter old man.'

'And you're still a scared little housewife.'

'Not just a housewife. A mother too.'

Takahashi lifted his pistol and the air cracked. His chest exploded and he slumped forward, gasping, his gun hanging from his fingertip.

'Where is my daughter?'

A pitter-patter of thick red circles hit the floor between Opere's feet. She reached up to her forehead and felt blood pouring from a wet, open wound. Dylan staggered towards her.

SEVENTY

D ylan caught her, and cradled her head in his hands. His palms were quickly slick with red. Opere's glassy eyes fixed on the ceiling, and her jaw twitched.

'Stay with me. Don't go.'

He laid her on the floor and checked her pulse, then her breath. A pool of crimson gathered below her neck.

Takahashi held his ripped chest and coughed. 'She was a prisoner of love … I set her free. She's gone.'

Dylan began chest compressions on Opere, but she slipped away from him, and he slumped at her side, exhausted.

'Love is a game that only one can win,' Takahashi said, wheezing now.

'Why aren't you dead?' Dylan shouted.

'I'm not afraid of dying, but only I know where Mika is … and if you want to see her again … you must keep me alive.'

SEVENTY-ONE

Takahashi ordered Dylan to get an emergency kit he'd stowed in the back room. Dylan picked up the shotgun, marched over to him, and pushed the muzzle against the old man's forehead.

'That's more like it,' Takahashi said. 'You're a killer after all.'

Dylan pulled the trigger.

The empty chamber clicked.

Takahashi smiled faintly. 'And now, such a strong will. But a little dim. Rule one. Always make sure you have the ammunition before you commit to a kill.'

A sharp pain lanced between Dylan's ribs.

'Such a stupid boy.'

Dylan looked down. A knife was pressing into his chest, not deep, not yet, but just enough to draw blood. Takahashi's blood-splattered hands grasped the hilt firmly.

'Tell me, if you had blown my head off, how would you have found Mika?' Takahashi twisted the dagger, then pulled it away. 'Go and get the medical kit.'

Dylan dropped the shotgun and stormed into the back room. It was full of junk – suitcases, money, laptops, passports. And … what the fuck? Cocaine.

'In the steel briefcase under the laptop,' Takahashi called out. 'Quickly. I'm—'

Dylan returned and threw the case open on the floor.

Takahashi gestured to the ground. 'Get me out of this chair.'

Dylan dragged him out of the chair and laid him down. Takahashi winced and his breathing became even more laboured. He pointed to a small vial of clear liquid.

'Diamorphine.' He nodded at his arm. 'Be careful with the dose … not too much.'

'How much?' Dylan said.

There was no response.

'Where's Mika?'

Takahashi's eyes closed and his body sagged. Dylan loaded a syringe half-full and plunged it into Takahashi's bicep. The man jolted and came to.

'Cut, cut …' Takahashi scissored his fingers over his shirt and beat the floor with his palm.

Dylan snipped away the cloth. Takahashi's chest was punctured by several deep wounds.

'Leave the fragments. Take out the larger pieces … bullet extractor …'

'What the hell did you say? I can hardly hear you! What's a bullet extractor?' Dylan rifled through the utensils. 'Is this it?' He held up a long, thin tool with a tiny retractable claw. Takahashi nodded.

Dylan hesitated over the largest wound, then pushed it in. Takahashi groaned, as Dylan dug around. After the third try, he tugged out a black ball.

Takahashi tensed and his eyes widened. 'Close the wound or my lung will collapse.' He slung his hand to the side and rummaged in the emergency kit, grasped an adhesive chest seal and thrust it into Dylan's hand. Dylan tore open the packet, wiped the trauma site and sealed the fleshy tear.

Takahashi breathed. 'That was too close … the painkillers are starting to kick in … Give me a mirror and bring me cocaine.'

He slipped out of consciousness and Dylan ran to the back and returned with a round mirror and a bag of white powder. He ripped it open, and Takahashi plunged his hand in, lifted his chalky fingertips to his nose and snorted.

'Prop my head up and hold the mirror. I won't survive your clumsy hands again.'

He slid the forceps into his abdomen and let out a desperate moan. Out came another chunk of buckshot. Two more times he did this. Then Dylan was ordered to stitch him up. He handed Dylan a needle and a packet of thick sutures.

Dylan threaded the implement and forced the thread through Takahashi's flesh. Takahashi raged at the poor workmanship, then barked instructions on how to clean and dress the injuries.

Within seconds of the last hole being patched, Dylan's presumptive father-in-law passed out.

SEVENTY-TWO

Takahashi lost consciousness, so Dylan used the time to search the shrine for Mika. He found statues, lanterns, a wall of prayers written on wooden plates, an offerings box and a set of garden tools. He checked the rooms and floors for fake walls and for trap doors. There were none. There was no Mika either.

Takahashi's possessions comprised suits and ties, hammers and knives, counterfeit travel documents and a single creased photograph of his daughter.

The man stirred, then coughed. His weak voice leaked through the door.

'I need blood.'

Dylan left the room and checked him. Strands of silver hair stuck to Takahashi's clammy face. He reached into the medical kit and pulled out a glass bottle, an empty IV bag, a tube and a set of instructions.

'Blood …'

'Tell me where Mika is.'

Takahashi shook his head. 'Fill this with her blood …' His pointed a trembling hand at Opere's corpse. 'Type-A … same as me … hurry.' He began to mumble incoherently and took another snort of cocaine. 'Make an incision … collect as much as you can.'

'No fucking way. I won't do that to Opere. She was right, you're just a bitter old man. Why don't you tell me where Mika is and die?'

'Mika's time is limited, like mine … But I'm not afraid. No grave can hold my body down.'

'You're dying alone, old man, just like your sister did. And you're going to take your daughter with you.'

Takahashi stiffened. 'I was once like you, full of love's false promises. You don't understand—'

'I know about Mika's illness. Who will be there for her now you're gone?'

Takahashi drifted and mumbled something. Dylan told him to repeat it.

'If I die, Mika will be trapped forever,' Takahashi said.

Dylan approached Opere's body, and for a moment, the clouding sensation crept up behind his eyes and his head began to throb.

'I'm so sorry,' he said. 'This is for Mika. I promise I'll find her.'

He pulled up Opere's shirt and pierced the discoloured skin at her flank. Blood spilled freely into the container. He transferred it to the IV bag and mounted it on Takahashi's wheelchair, then followed the instructional images, forcing the drip needle into Takahashi's forearm.

Blood began to flow through the tube. The old man's eyelids flickered. He spoke, his voice a mere whisper, and slipped out of consciousness.

SEVENTY-THREE

If you really knew her, you'd already know there's only one place I would put her . . .

What the hell did it mean?

Takahashi's breathing slowed, his chest moving only slightly.

Dylan slumped on the floor and tried to stitch his mind together, but the familiar feeling of a terrible future gathered pace behind his eyes with a high-pressure thump. His mind rewound to 2006. Geoff dying. Dylan helpless. His best friend reaching out across the floor, a bronze ring between his fingertips.

'Do it for those who can't,' Geoff had once said in a bar the first time they'd been assigned to work together. 'Stand up to the bullies of this world. That's how we get the A-grade at the Pearly Gates.'

Dylan marked his own work. F.

The park on the morning of the eleventh, the aura, Mika, her apartment, the quake, waiting for the water to come, the school and the fight for their lives, the language lessons Mika had given him.

Was that it? Was that the answer?

He sprinted out of the hall, down the path and under the torii gate. He slipped and fell, scrambled back to his feet, sweat stinging his eyes, blood staining his hands, his ribs protesting.

If he knew anything about Mika at all, it's that there was one place on earth she loved more than any other.

The school.

And if her father cared for her at all, that was where he'd have put her.

He raced up the stairs of the building, throat raw. Stopped and drew breath, letting his heart slow for a minute. Continued, dragging himself up each step. He checked every floor. Nothing.

At the top was a barricade of file cabinets, desks and a bookcase. He pulled them aside and into the corridor until the door was exposed. A note was attached to it. *Goddamn, I told the old man you'd find her. No hard feelings, pal – Shultz.*

Dylan pushed. It wouldn't budge. He leant his full weight against it. It give a little. A muffled voice came from within.

He yelled out Mika's name.

One more try.

He kicked.

The door gave.

Mika ran towards him and jumped into his arms. 'Is he dead?'

'Almost. Opere saved me. But I'm so sorry, Mika. She's gone. She was so brave, and she loved you so much.'

Mika doubled over and held herself for a moment. Then she righted herself, and through a stream of tears said, 'Take me to her.'

SEVENTY-FOUR

The door of the worship hall framed her father's empty wheelchair. Mika paused in the long shadow cast by the lion dogs, frozen with guilt. White clouds moved fast across the sky and the red timber of the temple no longer suggested harmony. Her soul burned.

'If I don't go in, maybe they'll still be alive. In my heart at least. It'd be easier to pretend this never happened.' She put her hands on her cheeks. 'I don't have to accept this. I don't have to admit they're gone. Would it be so wrong to live a lie?'

'They'll always be in your heart, Mika. I don't blame you if you don't want to go in. It's too much to see in there. You shouldn't see her like this. Don't let this picture define your mother's memory.'

'All I have are ghosts.' She wiped her tears with her bandaged hand. 'But if I don't go inside, I'll regret not seeing them one last time.'

She bowed and crossed the threshold. Dylan stayed at her back.

Her parents lay in separate pools of blood that had almost run together. Mika stood between them and wept for the irreversible brutality of it all. This was a tragedy that had no cure, and all the good energy in the world couldn't bring her mother back.

Mika took her mother's cold hand and kissed it. 'Too soon.'

To her father, her feelings were less pure. She stared over him, stony faced. 'You had the power of life, and all you wanted to do was crush it. You got what you deserve.'

Takahashi stirred. 'Mika …' Strands of cocaine-stained silver hair stuck to his cold, clammy face.

'Are you in pain?' Mika said, her voice cold.

He nodded and mumbled something Mika couldn't make out.

'He's saying diamorphine,' Dylan said. 'It's the liquid in that vial. It's a painkiller.'

Mika loaded the used syringe halfway.

'That's enough,' Dylan said. 'That's how much he had earlier. He said you have to be careful with the dose.'

She paused, then filled the chamber and pushed the needle into her father's arm. 'No more suffering, Papa. Not for any of us.'

The old man grew older. His topless, patched-up torso and his stump of a leg was stained full red. His silver hair, muddled and messy, was marked crimson too. With a groan, the tension and agony dropped from his face and he appeared to find peace.

'Let's go. We've desecrated this place enough,' Mika said.

They walked across the gravel and blossom path towards the torii gate.

'There is something you need to hear,' Dylan said. 'Something your parents kept from you … to protect you.'

Mika raised her hand. 'Stop!'

'I'm sorry to hit you with this now, but you have to know this. You—'

'I know,' Mika said. 'The doctor called with the blood test results yesterday morning. He told me.'

She took Dylan's hand. He'd told her something else too.

She was pregnant.

SEVENTY-FIVE

A pack of playful Akitas jumped up at Nao.

'Hey there, fellas. Fine weather today, isn't it?'

He scooped a frying pan into a sack tied to his bike trailer and laid piles of food on the road.

'There you go. Plenty for everyone.'

He picked up a pup and tickled its furry blonde belly.

'Hi, boy. My name's Nao. We shall call you Goosey. A fine name for a playful young man.' He set the wriggling puppy down by his mother.

An engine whined a little way off.

'And who do we have now? More hungry mouths?'

A Super Cub rolled up beside the dogs. On it were Mika the schoolteacher and Dylan the Englishman, both looking worse for wear.

'What are you doing back here? What happened to you both?'

'Nao! I'm so glad to see you,' Dylan said.

'Your Japanese has improved!'

'We were just headed to your house,' Mika said. 'We didn't know where else to go. Some terrible things have happened.' She burst into tears.

Nao nodded. 'Come with me. Follow me home.' He pointed at Dylan. 'For you, I have Saké. And for you' – he took Mika's hand –

'Yoshi will be glad to see you.'

She told her story by the fire, Yoshi in her lap. Dylan sipped from his tumbler.

'Too many problems,' Nao said. 'Too much tragedy.' He took a deep breath. 'I'm sorry for everything, Mika. You've been through so much and nearly met your end. But at some point there has to be a new beginning. Remember, your life is more than these moments of pain. Before you realise, the future will have arrived and life will be good again. Try to celebrate your mother's life. And know that you both can stay here until you're strong again.'

SEVENTY-SIX

The pain was a fire, but the seasons passed, and Mika and Dylan left Nao and headed north once again, to where the shade grew thick under trees and the early-morning sun dazzled.

'Here,' Dylan said. 'This is where she brought me.'

'I didn't realise it was so far from the house,' Mika said, catching her breath. 'It really is beautiful here. I can see why she loved this place.'

Dylan pointed to the tall, slender red-crowned cranes. They paraded and frolicked, just like when Opere had brought him to this clearing months earlier.

'It's perfect,' Mika said.

A thick mist rose from the grass in a haze, as the sun rose, a phantasm of orange and blue.

Mika pulled a glazed pewter urn from out of her rucksack and held it up to the light. 'Look, Mom. I can see why the lakes and birds were so special to you. There are so many cranes here today! They all want to welcome you back home. Some are dancing. I think the males are trying to impress the ladies with their wings, but the females don't seem very impressed.' Mika wiped her cheek. 'I really wish we could have come here together, just once.'

She took the heavy top off the container.

'I know you'll be happier here than anywhere else in the world, and me and Dylan will come and see you all the time. You were the best mom a daughter could have. I wish I'd told you that … I miss you. I'll love you, forever. And I will never forget you.'

As tears choked her, she emptied Opere's ashes into the delicate morning wind.

SEVENTY-SEVEN

Almost nine months after Dylan's collapse in Yonomori Park, he and Mika touched down at Heathrow. Journalists greeted them with a flash of cameras and a barrage of questions.

'Dylan, what are your plans now?'

'Can you tell our readers how you survived?'

'Where exactly have you been all this time?'

'Is that your wife? Is she carrying your baby?'

'Can you respond to the allegations made against your former editor, Sam MacLaine?'

'What do you make of Jushin Okada's escape?'

Mika smiled and leant in towards his ear. 'Are you sure about this?'

'I want our little girl to be brought into a better world,' he whispered. 'So, yeah, I'm sure.'

Dylan and Mika pushed through the horde of reporters towards the black, chauffeur-driven Mercedes Benz laid on by his publisher.

He turned to the crowd. 'I'll make a statement in due time.'

They climbed in, and the car pulled away. London rolled by – its shops, buses, traffic and noise.

Mika cradled her belly. 'I want to call her Opere.'

Dylan took her hand and smiled. The name was perfect.

SEVENTY-EIGHT

The man in a tuxedo teased open a golden envelope, leaned into the bright lights and spoke into a microphone.

'And the winner of the 2012 Courage in Journalism award goes to … Dylan Solly!'

The audience roared as Dylan made his way up red-carpeted steps to the stage, then settled as he took hold of the crystal globe and approached the lectern.

He looked down at the trophy. 'When you get an award like this, you're usually at the end of your career and about a week away from claiming your pension.'

The crowd tittered.

'In all seriousness, it's an honour to receive this. I know that's what you're supposed to say, but it's true. Of all the dangerous places my work's taken me over the years, none have made me feel as nervous as stepping up here and talking to you lot.'

In front of him, a sea of faces. All jolly and drunk.

'I want to dedicate this award to my partner and soon-to-be wife, Mika, and our child, Opere, who's due any day now.'

The audience cheered once more, and a picture of Mika, heavily pregnant and dressed in summer blue, came on screen.

'Violet, where is she?' Dylan shaded his eyes from the lights. 'There she is! Thank you, Violet. You were an ally during tough times. You're also the best researcher I've ever worked with, and I look forward to more projects with you in the years to come.'

The clapping rose and fell.

'And since my former editor, Sam MacLaine, is currently detained at Her Majesty's Pleasure, she'd probably prefer it if I don't mention her at all, and that's fine with me.'

Laughter now.

Dylan cleared his throat. 'Geoff, an old friend of mine that some of you may remember, once told me that it's our duty to stand up for the unrepresented, for the repressed and the abused. I wouldn't be the man I am if it wasn't for his example.' Dylan looked to the sky. 'Thanks, G.'

He gripped the lectern and let a wave of applause die down.

'As journalists, we always look for the hot angle, for that one killer line that reveals the essence of the story. Sometimes it's elusive, sometimes it only comes out when you're drunk, and sometimes it's stuck in your head when you're trying to sleep.'

He took a breath.

'The world needs more than love. That phrase has been rattling around my brain for months. Because it feels true, doesn't it? Has love done enough for us? For the starving families across the world, for domestic abuse victims, for victims of racism? Has it stopped cruelty towards animals, or helped the generations who've been wiped out by genocide, or the people who died crossing borders trying to escape persecution, or the millions of victims suffering from abuses of power across the globe? Has love done enough for them? No, it hasn't. Because love was never meant to stand alone. Love needs an army. It needs courage. So never forget to be brave, not just for yourself but for those around you. Only together can we make this world better.

'Thank you, members of the panel. I treasure this award. And I have one final thing to say to you before I go. Tomorrow, do just one thing to make the world better, one meaningful gesture to help your neighbour or a family member or a work colleague. Maybe pick up the phone and check in on someone who might need a friendly voice. It needn't be huge. And it needn't cost anything, but it'll still be worth more than you know. Until then, let's get pissed and have the best night ever!'

EPILOGUE

Superintendent Usami brushed the fringe from his eyes. 'I understand, Commissioner.'

'And you understand how this reflects on the entire police force?'

'I do.'

'You were very quick to claim glory for Jushin Okada's capture, and now he's escaped what are you going to do?'

'Intelligence says he's fled the country. He might be trying to track down the man who aided his capture, so with your permission I'll follow Okada to London.'

'And once you're in England?'

'I'll try to find him before he kills Dylan Solly.'

Thank you for reading *Mika Ito*! There is more to come from our star-crossed couple in 2023. But if you've enjoyed this, I think you'd like to meet Drew and Hazel, the stars of my debut novel *The Shelter*, it's an exciting thriller and it's out now. **Turn the page to find out more.**

THE SHELTER

You think you're safe. You're wrong.

OUT NOW

The Shelter is a tense and completely gripping thriller. It's the perfect read for fans of authors like T.M. Logan, David Baldacci and Alex Marwood. Available in eBook and paperback.

You think you're safe. You're wrong. When an unusual category five hurricane threatens to devastate California, it forces five strangers to seek shelter inside a woodland bunker. But the bunker is already occupied.

Pastor Quincy Gordon has claimed it as a sanctuary for his church. He welcomes the visitors, but as the storm rages, he locks the entrance, trapping everyone inside.

Soon, the five will wish they'd taken their chances outside with Mother Nature, because what lurks within the shelter is far more sinister...

Turn the page to read the first chapter...

THE SHELTER – CHAPTER ONE

THE LAST PLANE BACK TO PARADISE

B reathe.

This is a contentious story. It's a story of possibilities and improbabilities, of decisions and change, of the moments, both powerful and forced, that pave the path to catastrophe.

You might be on this path, but don't worry, you're sure to find company. I know of at least five people heading towards disaster right now. Drew Samuel is one of them. He's thirty-two, slight build, average height, with loosely curled flaxen hair and tired olive-colored eyes. He's currently on an airplane, dressed as he usually is – in sandals, red beach shorts, an orange T-shirt, and a wool-lined denim jacket.

He's a DJ, although the days of hit songs, arena crowds, and cramped after show parties are behind him. Now, he's got uncharted albums, tiny festival stages, and Bobby, his long-serving manager of dubious repute.

Drew's future isn't set yet, but the declines of his recent past have delivered him to an unenviable present. In other words, the rigors of the road have broken his spirit. I don't know if his courage will return, but I do know this: if he maintains his seat on this airplane, a dangerous series of events will unfold.

Drew's hungover and his flight is delayed. He's made it to his seat, but his condition is deteriorating. While lively passengers mutter, he melts. Beads of sweat gather on his brow as he looks back at the last twelve hours of his life with regret.

Somebody shoot me. When will I learn? Vodka is evil... Peace and tranquility, please, God, give me peace and tranquility.

Desperate for relief from the rising cabin temperature, he reaches a trembling arm to the ceiling panel and twists the serrated air nozzle. It exhales hot air.

"Excuse me, sir," a voice says over his shoulder, "I'm afraid that can't take up a whole seat. Please stow it in the overhead compartment."

Drew flinches. *Please, no...*

Memories flash and distract: his fingers wrapped around a glass bottle, the sound of sloshing and the taste of concentrate. He blinks himself upright, banishing the caustic images, and his vision settles on a flight attendant. She's small, round, and brilliant red. A white scarf hangs from one side of her hat and tucks into her neckline somewhere. Drew can't fathom it.

The scarf? Where does it go?

He stares at her wrinkled uniform.

"Sir, stow that away, please," she says.

He wonders what she means.

Why's she so annoyed? Oh, wait, no. That. It can only be that.

Strapped into the seat next to him is a two-foot, plinth-mounted microphone with the words "**Worst DJ of 2021**" etched on the base. It absorbs his attention.

Thanks, BundaFestival, you smart-arse. I bet Bobby put you up to that.

Reality reaches him in waves, waves that smash into a million drops and scatter. His eyes wander around the plane. Passengers peek back at him.

"Sir, sir? Are you listening?" The flight attendant is not letting this go.

"I'm sorry," he says, "but I really, really want to go home."

A few passengers snigger.

Drew nods. Now he understands. Now he knows what must be done. He must stow his dubious prize in the overhead locker. *Certainly. Of course.*

He fumbles at the inscrutably smooth seat belt clip but fails to decipher its suddenly elaborate design. He pulls at its heavy nylon straps.

What's going on here? Help. Why isn't this working?

Confounded by the clinking metal, he's trapped in his chair.

"What a mess!" shouts a passenger, and others agree. Brash sneers and other antagonisms, deliberately not whispered, trample and bruise. Time distorts. The waves in Drew's mind become a stormy sea, and the flight attendant presses the issue again.

"Sir, if you can't stow that away, I'm going to call security and have you escorted off the plane."

He gasps for air. Everyone is looking and it's so hot in here – hard to breathe. Footsteps come up the aisle, he fears the worst until a familiar smile appears, and a crack of laughter breaks the tide.

"Thank God," Drew mumbles into his hands.

"Don't worry, my lovely," Bobby says to the flight attendant.

Bobby's older than Drew, yet somehow, he exudes a vitality that Drew doesn't. It's thanks in part to his smile. Bobby flashes the crowd a full-contact grin, complete with sharp teeth, fleshy gums, and glinting sea-blue eyes.

No one can weaponize a smile like Bobby. He'd have made a fantastic pirate.

"I'm sorry I'm late," Bobby says. "Don't worry, ma'am. I'm this man's manager. Allow me to deal with this." Bobby crouches to Drew's eye level.

"Hey, Drew. Drew? Your award's going in the overhead, okay? You haven't been the same since Berlin, have you, lad, but don't worry, it's been a long three months, but the tour's over and you're going home, yeah?"

Drew feels a slow, leery frown pour out of his face. Bobby stows away Drew's ill-advised metal mascot and turns to the flight attendant.

"I'm so sorry, dear, it's clear what's happened here – this man has had a bad oyster. The flight will do him good."

She rolls her eyes and walks down the aisle.

"What would I do without you, Bobby, my fine Irish friend?" Drew stumbles over his words. "For the last ten years, what would I have done? I'd have probably been happy and sober, I expect."

Bobby takes his seat next to Drew and leans in close, "Come on, lad. The way you behave, you'd be in the rubber room or locked up someplace without me."

"Bollocks. This is all your fault. I blame you, your stupid tour, your stupid award – and your awful vodka. Why do you always get me into this mess?"

"Sounds like you want another bottle, pal!" Bobby slaps his leg and bursts into laughter. "Some DJ you are. Mr. Superstar, my arse! You should just be grateful we got on this flight. After ten years of service as your manager, it doesn't hurt to say thanks once in a while."

"Thanks for the last ten years of shitty economy flights and arse-hole-of-nowhere festivals and generally career-ending shit bookings, *Bobby*," Drew leers.

"Don't mention it."

Drew sighs.

"And you should be extra thankful for this particular flight. You know my brother's a pilot, right? Well, he's been briefed that all flights to California are being grounded as of tomorrow. A hurricane's due in – Hurricane Jason – and it's going to be a big one, so we have to get home and batten down the hatches until it passes."

"A hurricane in California? You're full of crap, Bobby." Drew nods again until another wave of vodka rears up at him.

More mutters and sniggers from the other passengers, but Drew can't hear them now. He pushes himself deep into the chair's smooth squeaky leather.

It's finally over. After three months, no more tour buses, no more flights, no more half-empty festivals, no more Bobby, and definitely no more eastern European booze. Just this one plane ride and it's all over. I've finally made it.

The plane thrusts down the tarmac and lifts Drew into a cloudless night. He tries to banish a harsh ringing from his ears. In 30,000 feet of sky, he blinks himself into a turbulent sleep. At five hundred miles an hour, he flies unconscious into the eye of a new storm.

The Shelter is available on Amazon now

And please sign up to my newsletter at https://peterfoley.co.uk to find out more about my upcoming books and follow me on social media @thepeterfoley. See you there!

AFTERWORD

W ell, I hope you enjoyed that. Writing an afterword is always difficult: there are always so many people to thank and this is such an impersonal way of doing it. But here goes. You're the first person on my list, no doubt, so thank you for taking the time and indulging me in letting me tell my latest story. Thanks for buying it, and if you've told your friends or left a review (5 stars, ahem), then extra thanks are certainly in order.

And thank you, as ever, to my wife, Helen, who put up with me while I obsessed over this story's plot for way too long. She also put up with me texting her lists of possible book titles at random moments in any given day, when we were struggling to find the right one. Along the way, Clare Coombes at Liverpool Literacy Agency gave me some great advice (and some of her precious time), which I really appreciated. Johanna Sartori's feedback was also essential. As was Helen Varley and Tom May's advice on the book cover design, their input was valuable. Agata Broncel over at www.bukovero.com did an amazing job with the artwork, I couldn't be happier with it. Thank you for coming up with my dream cover. And Louise Harnby (www.louiseharnbyproofreader.com), thanks for the terrific edit which really lifted the MS, and Kim Kimber (kimkimber.co.uk) and Peri Turner for their superb skills at spotting my many typos. Rachael and Nat www.thebooktypesetters.com really did an awesome job.

A special note to all my family and friends who took the time to ask me how my book career was going when it was down in the dumps. Your enthusiasm helped me along.

I've spent a year writing this story, and if you want to tell me that you liked the book, and you have other nice things to say, please get in touch @thepeterfoley. You can also find me at www.peterfoley.co.uk.

Just a reminder before I go: without an Amazon or a Goodreads review, I'm basically toast. I don't have the luxury of being a full-time writer. Like many others, I work a day job. Writing full time is a pipe dream. One day, maybe I'll get to be one of the lucky club who gets to hang out with my characters all day. I hope so, but I can't get there without you, so I hope you come along for the ride as I continue to develop my career. So if you can, please drop a 5-star on me. I appreciate it.

P.S. Oh, before I go, I have a companion novella that complements the *Mika Ito* novel. It takes place during the same timeline as Mika Ito, it's called *Mika Ito: Red Shift* and tells the story from the bad guys point of view, and that of the other supporting cast. How did Shinsuke survive the tsunami? Who rescued him? When and how?

Mika Ito: Red Shift novella is planned for release in late 2022. It'll be on Amazon, probably as an eBook only offering. Check out www.peterfoley.co.uk to find out more, and find me on social media at @thepeterfoley.

A NOTE FROM THE PUBLISHER

Thank you for reading this book. If you enjoyed it please do consider leaving a review on Amazon to help others find it too.

Also, **I hate typos**. This book has been rigorously edited and proofread, but sometimes mistakes do slip through. If you have spotted a typo, please do let me and I'll get it amended.

peter@peterfoley.co.uk
www.peterfoley.co.uk
@thepeterfoley